THE ISLAND TYCOON

Edwina Rosewall and her flighty sister Julia couldn't have been less alike—but Damon Morven chose to think Edwina was as bad as her sister, and took it out on her accordingly. So when he began to show signs of wanting to ruin the unspoiled Bahamian island where she was working so happily, Edwina was ready to do battle!

THE ISLAND TYCOON

BY
JANE CORRIE

MILLS & BOON LIMITED
15–16 BROOK'S MEWS
LONDON W1A 1DR

First published 1984

© Jane Corrie 1984

Australian copyright 1984

ISBN 0 263 10511 3

Set in 11 on 12½ pt Linotron Times
07–0484–47,000

*Photoset by Rowland Phototypesetting Ltd
Bury St Edmunds, Suffolk
Made and printed in Great Britain by
Richard Clay (The Chaucer Press) Ltd
Bungay, Suffolk*

CHAPTER ONE

EDWINA ROSEWALL stood behind the reception desk of the Splendour and waited for the latest arrivals to the luxury hotel on the small island that was one of a group that made up the Bahama out-islands.

Her brown eyes with the tawny flecks in them wore a soft wholly satisfied expression. From where she stood she could see the breakers making foaming white encroachments on the sandy beach. To her right, the fronds of a palm tree swayed gently in the breeze.

Six months ago, she had been teaching at a Surrey college, with only vague memories of her early life spent in the sunny Caribbean, where her father had had the post of secretary to the British Consul, Sir Charles Taylor. She was seven years old when the Consul had retired and returned to the U.K., taking most of his staff with him, her father included, for he had been offered the post of private secretary to Sir Charles, who, far from resting from his distinguished diplomatic career, had decided to write his memoirs.

The whole family had returned to England. Edwina, her sister Julia, who at that time was just three, soon settled down, as did their parents, on Sir Charles's country estate, Mrs Rosewall only

5

digging her heels in when a living-in post was suggested, for she preferred the privacy of family life, and they had been allotted the old lodge, only a few minutes' walk from the Manor House.

It was through Julia that Edwina owed her present very agreeable change of scenery. It was shortly after Julia's twentieth birthday that she had declared that she wanted to see the world, and when Julia set her mind on something, that was the end of the matter.

The trouble was that Julia was spoilt. A petite blonde, with more than her share of good looks, with huge blue eyes that could wring your heart out, depending on what she was angling for, she rarely failed to gain her victory for whatever cause she had embarked on, a cause that was invariably aimed at self-achievement.

It would not be entirely fair to suggest that Mrs Rosewall had a favourite daughter, but it was true that she appeared to understand Julia's temperament a little better than she understood Edwina's. The same went for Mr Rosewall, only he did understand Edwina, and had little sympathy for the whims and tantrums of his younger daughter, much preferring the company of Edwina, who would help him when the work got burdensome and who would type up reams of research for him to ease the load.

After a few warning shots across the prow of the family ship at present sailing in calm seas, Julia suddenly announced her intention of joining some friends of hers on a safari excursion to the middle of nowhere, and a worried Mrs Rosewall, who quite definitely disapproved of these particular friends, had had to come up with an alternative scheme to dissuade her wilful daughter from doing any such thing.

With the connections the Rosewalls had in the Caribbean, it was a natural and safer choice to bring to Julia's attention, and added to that the fact that Peter Knight, a distant relation on Mr Rosewall's side, had a hotel on one of the out-islands, it was, for Mrs Rosewall, the better of the two evils, for motherlike, she did not want her flock straying from the fold, and she was sure she could rely on Peter to look out for the two girls—for she had decided that Edwina should go along too, as an added guardian over Julia's 'high spirits', as she put it, only Mr Rosewall and Edwina had another name for it.

A few weeks earlier Edwina would have refused such an undertaking, but since she was then going through the trauma of a broken engagement, anywhere was preferable from the places that only held poignant memories for her. In point of fact, it was quite possible that she would have accompanied Julia on her safari trip without a backward thought.

Edwina came out of her reverie to check in the few guests and murmur a welcoming greeting as she handed them their keys; she watched the porters take over the luggage and shepherd them to the lift, then with a satisfied sigh, got back to her musings again.

She still could not believe how well things had turned out, and that she was now free from worry where Julia was concerned, but at the start of their arrival things had not looked too good for her, for Julia, being Julia, had decided that she was not going to stay at Cousin Peter's hotel, declaring that she was not going to be spied on, and how he would report back home all their doings, and after all, that was what she had left home for, etc.; and she had taken herself off to a much larger island that offered more scope in the entertainment line, and probably more chance of work, for here again Julia flatly refused to work in Peter's hotel, for more or less the same reasons.

With their past connections, and with Peter's sponsoring, it had not been hard for the girls to get work permits, since neither of them had any intention of presuming on Peter's goodwill.

Julia, with her secretarial training, and her past work in an accountants' office, that would not have lasted very long, since she played havoc with the articled clerks' emotions, would not have found it hard to find a job, and Edwina's past teaching experience, plus her office work for her father, also entitled her to find a position, so there had been no worries there, but Edwina was inclined to agree with Julia that it would be better if they did not work for Peter, only for different reasons. Peter might not need more help, but might feel obliged to create some sort of a position for them, and that was unfair.

As the arrangements had already been made for the girls to stay at Peter's hotel, Edwina had to go ahead with that part of the arrangement, leaving

Julia to make her own arrangements, which she did, within an hour of them landing on the island. At least Edwina had managed to make Julia accompany her to see Peter, and give her own excuses as to why she had decided to take herself off, accepted, much to Edwina's surprise, with an aplomb that she had not credited her cousin with, and that made Edwina rethink her earlier assessment of Peter Knight, whom she had always regarded as a shy, rather introverted character who appeared to have no interests other than his hotel, a born bachelor, in fact, and who went so far as to provide Julia with an address of a good hotel, even approving of her choice of island and remarking in his stilted way of talking that she would find more in the way of entertainment there.

Peter, Edwina thought, after Julia had gone her way, accompanied by one of Peter's employees to see to her luggage and see her on to one of the ferries, was not such an old slouch after all, and must have gained some insight into Julia's tempestuous character during his once a year visit to the U.K., and the Rosewalls, the only relations he had left.

Edwina knew him to be thirty-five, yet for all his manncrisms one would have thought him older, so set in his ways was he, but somewhere behind those thick hornrimmed spectacles and bland features, there obviously lurked a self-protective mechanism where girls like Julia were concerned. But Edwina was not too certain that this did not apply to her, too, and the first thing she did after settling in at the hotel was to tell Peter that she intended to get herself a job, hastily assuring him that she was not cadging one from him, but maybe he could suggest something she could do.

To her amazement Peter had shown a definite disinclination for her abrupt removal, even appearing to be a little hurt that she should consider moving out so quickly, and there was time enough to work something out, and why shouldn't she just enjoy herself for a few weeks and maybe something would turn up, some staff shortage or other. It was a small island, he reminded her, and there were only three hotels on the island.

With her fears of being an incumbent on Peter quashed, Edwina was only too pleased to follow his advice, and she spent the next fortnight gaining a suntan and generally lazing around, but at the back of her mind there always lurked the worry of what Julia was getting up to, although she had regular reports from her by phone, and not even the fact that Julia had landed herself a job within three days of landing on the island of her choice, as a receptionist in one of the swanky hotels, had completely removed this worry.

A fortnight's lazing was enough for Edwina, and when Peter mentioned a job that he had heard was going at the Splendour, the largest and most luxurious hotel on the island, Edwina, armed with references and Peter's endorsement, applied for the post as secretary to the manager of the hotel, which she obtained, much to her delight.

During the next six weeks she settled into the

work, which she found congenial and wholly satisfying. She was very busy, and had no time to worry about Julia. She had moved into the hotel at the manager's suggestion, for Peter's hotel was on the other side of the island, and meant a thirty-minute ride over roads that badly needed repairing, not to mention the transport situation. As the manager, Mr Rider, had pointed out, the most sensible solution was that she took the room vacated by his last secretary.

Everything was fine. Edwina was able to report home with glowing accounts of how well things were going for them, and how Julia was enjoying herself, for going by her enthusiastic accounts of her outings, and the escorts available, Julia was having the time of her life.

Edwina had always meant to slip over to the island one day on her off duty periods, and give Julia a surprise, but somehow she had never got around to it, for she had gone to Peter's hotel in a much quieter section of the island, that catered mainly for the fishing fraternity of the holiday-makers, out after marlins, unlike the Splendour, that catered for the idle rich who wanted, and got, everything on tap, including indoor swimming pools, and every type of entertainment needed to supply the perfect holiday. Although Edwina enjoyed her work, it was a place she was glad to escape from on her off-duty periods. The hustle and bustle of the frantically busy staff made it impossible for her to relax in comfort anywhere else but her room, and so she had chosen the

Haven, Peter's hotel, precisely for what it was.

It all seemed too good to be true, and of course it was. Julia arrived back suddenly one evening, bag and baggage and all, declaring she had had enough of 'that pesky place'.

Edwina had no idea what had happened to make Julia suddenly pull up sticks and move on, but with Julia you really didn't need a reason. She could have just got bored with her surroundings and decided to move on, so Edwina did not enquire too closely into the reason for her abrupt departure; she was more worried about what to do about Julia now that she was footloose and raring to go elsewhere.

Grand Bahama had been mentioned, and it was plain that this time Julia expected Edwina to go with her, and Edwina had no wish to leave her present employment. She had tasted life without the encumbrance of her wilful younger sister, and was not looking forward to resuming the position of guardian again.

To make matters worse, Peter had been lecturing Julia on her behaviour to the staff at the Haven, and suggested that she do a little more for herself and not expect everybody to wait upon her, for they were at the height of the season, and although it was a small hotel, it was exclusive, and the type of guest they catered for expected value for money. They were paying enough for it, for fishing was the sport of kings in that region and only the very rich could afford to indulge in it.

Edwina's musings were interrupted by a young couple who had been wandering idly about the reception lobby and then came towards her and enquired where the swimming pool was. She directed them to a sign at the end of the long lobby that pointed to the entertainments area.

It was such a huge concern that half the receptionist's time was taken up by such enquiries until the guests found their way around. It had taken Edwina a few days herself to find her way around, but she did think it was a good idea to have the reception area completely cut off from the main centre of the hotel. Here, it was always quiet and orderly, and guests could make their enquiries without feeling they were making a nuisance of themselves.

All was peace again as the couple moved off, and Edwina, knowing that no influx was expected until the four o'clock flight landed, by which time two receptionists whom she had relieved for a brief spell would be back on duty, went happily back to her musings.

If it hadn't been for Stanley P. Nelson the Third, things might have been very different, and Edwina would not still be at the Splendour, for it was certain that Julia's departure was imminent, and that went for Edwina too, in spite of Peter's annoyed comment that Julia was old enough to look after herself and not to let her push Edwina into doing something she did not want to do. However, Stanley Nelson had appeared on the scene, and like so many before him had been bowled over by Julia's beauty, and being rich and fancy-free, had proposed, and been accepted by

Julia within the space of a month. Stanley's money came from oil, lots of it, inherited from his father, and Edwina had no qualms from the monetary angle, although she did like Stanley. It was the speed of things that she had not felt too easy about—but here again Peter had settled her worries. He had known Stanley Nelson for several years, for he had been a guest at his hotel until he had decided to take a place of his own, so the acquaintance was of long standing.

'He's not all that much older than Julia. In any case, she needs an older man to curb her exuberance,' Peter had said, when Edwina had voiced her worries to him.

The wedding took place in England and was held in the small chapel on Sir Charles Taylor's estate, and of course Edwina attended, going back home with the happy couple and returning on an earlier flight on her own, leaving the couple, or rather Stanley, to get acquainted with his in-laws.

Edwina's only sorrow at that time had been leaving her father, for as he had pointed out, there was really no need for her to return. Julia was settled, and although she would be returning to the Bahamas with her husband, he saw no reason why Edwina should go back.

It was a chance remark made by her mother that had settled things for her, for she had told Edwina that Philip had been asking after her, and the look that had accompanied this news, a look that had said, 'I'm sure that it's going to be all right now,' had Edwina checking on her return flight.

Philip Cawshaw had been her fiancé, an up-and-coming dental surgeon, whom Edwina had caught kissing Julia at a dance, and it had not been a brotherly kiss either, for they had wandered out into the grounds of the house for purely amorous intentions. Not that Edwina blamed Julia—in fact, when she had calmed down and looked at things perceptively, she knew that she had saved her from making a big mistake. It would have been too late after the wedding to have found out that her husband had a roving eye, and all the misery that that would entail in the years to come.

Precisely a week after the wedding, Edwina returned to the Bahamas, and her job at the Splendour. Julia and her husband would be following in a few weeks' time, with Julia grandly inviting Edwina to spend all her free time at the villa, Stanley's home on the island—an invitation that Edwina was not too keen to accept, for she much preferred to stick to her usual routine and go to the Haven.

That was three months ago, and Edwina, now free from worry, had settled down to her job again. She had visited Julia once or twice in her new home, and been amused by Julia's nonchalant acceptance of the luxury that surrounded her, and one would have thought that she was born to it. She had, of course, been spoilt and waited upon all her life, but even so, not quite to the extent she was now.

She was so caught up in her new life that she did not miss Edwina, and for that Edwina was grateful, because it left her off-times free, and although she did grumble once or twice at Edwina's constant refusal to make up a dinner party, she did not make a big thing out of it, since all Stanley's acquaintances were high-powered business executives, and there was no shortage of numbers to make up the dinner parties, and Edwina suspected that it was at Stanley's bidding that Julia threw out the odd invitation.

It had all worked out extremely well, Edwina thought happily, and smiled at the man who had just entered the reception lobby, thinking that he must have got held up somewhere, for the other guests had been checked in, and were by now well settled in. He was too early for the four o'clock flight, for a quick glance at the ornate clock on the opposite wall told her it was just three-thirty. He had been anxious to examine the facilities of the island, she thought, and had not bothered to check in before now, although she did wonder where his luggage was, for he carried only a briefcase.

The second thought that he was probably a travel agent come to make arrangements flitted through her mind as he approached the desk, but was gone as soon as she noted the autocratic bearing of the man, and the tailor-made beautifully cut suit of lightweight grey twill, and her hand automatically went towards the reservation book as she waited for the man to give his name.

'You don't need that,' the man said, clipping his words in a fashion that made Edwina feel that she ought to drop him a curtsey. 'Is Mr Rider in his office?' he queried.

'Yes—sir,' Edwina replied, adding the 'sir' hesitantly. She had heard that some guests liked that address, and those that didn't soon told you so, but not this one, she thought, as the man turned abruptly in the direction of the manager's office.

Before he reached it, however, something occurred to him and he wheeled round and stared at Edwina. 'Have I seen you before somewhere?' he asked.

Edwina blinked. It was the way the question had been asked that had startled her, for it was almost an accusation and not a query. 'Not to my knowledge,' she replied truthfully. She had seen a lot of people since she had been on the island, but she was certain that she had never seen this man before.

The more she thought about it, the more certain she was. She would not have forgotten a man like him, she mused idly—his six feet height, and cold good-looking features, with dark brown hair and grey eyes to match the forbidding exterior. No, she wouldn't have forgotten meeting him.

'Are you sure?' the man persisted, still in that accusing manner. 'What's your name?' he barked out at her.

'Edwina Rosewall,' Edwina replied, now ready to take offence at his manner.

'I thought so!' the man replied quickly, and stalked off to the manager's office, leaving a slightly stunned Edwina staring after him.

Was the man mad? she thought. Ought she to ring for Joel Coach, the security man? The manager might need help any minute now, she thought, as she saw the man go straight into the office without bothering to knock.

She was saved from her dilemma by the return of the two receptionists, laughing and talking over some party they had been to the night before, and managed to bring back some sense of normality for Edwina, who thought she had possibly over-reacted, and the man didn't look like a criminal, or even unbalanced. It was probably a coincidence, and in time all would be ironed out.

From her office adjoining the manager's room, she would be able to keep an eye on things, she told herself, for should any altercation be taking place, then all she had to do was to summon the house detective. Should she have had to pass through the manager's room to enter hers, then she would have waited outside, and not dared to enter, but as it was, her room, although adjoining the manager's, was completely separate, in order to afford the manager complete privacy.

There was no need for Edwina to strain to hear what was being said in the next room, for shouted would be a better word—not by Mr Rider, who had a mild unassuming voice, but by the hard voice of the stranger.

'I want her out of here, do you hear? I don't care how good her references are. They're probably working some kind of a con game, and I'm taking no chances, and that's an end to it!'

Edwina's eyebrows raised at this. Well, whoever the man had got it in for, it couldn't be her, she thought calmly, and thought that she had probably got there too late to hear whatever he had said to the manager regarding her, and why he should have adopted that attitude towards her.

A thoroughly unpleasant man, she concluded, before getting back to her work after a few minutes of peace had reigned in the office next door, and that meant that whoever he was, he had left.

Five minutes later, Edwina received her notice from a very apologetic and very embarrassed manager.

'I don't pretend to understand what's going on, Miss Rosewall,' he said, with a nervous cough, 'but I have strict instructions to remove you from the staff forthwith.' He coughed again. 'I am entirely at a loss to know precisely why. All I can say is that Mr Morven—er—that's the gentleman who has just called on me, and who has just become the proprietor of the hotel, insists on your removal.'

Edwina stared at him. She had never experienced being given the sack before. It was not a pleasant happening, and it wasn't as if she had done anything wrong. 'I've never seen that man before in my life,' she said indignantly. 'It's obviously a case of mistaken identity, and he might have waited until things were straightened out,' she added angrily.

The manager shook his head slowly. 'Not in this case, I'm afraid,' he said quietly. 'It appears that he's already had some dealings with a relation of yours. He also owns the Calypso,' he added significantly, and gave another dry cough. 'I believe you had a sister working there?'

Edwina's angry flush was replaced by a shocked white that blanched the peach tan that she had acquired. 'Julia isn't a criminal either,' she said haughtily.

The manager spread his hand in a helpless gesture. 'I'm very sorry, Miss Rosewall, I only wish there was something that I could do, but as it is—'

Edwina nodded her head abruptly. 'Thank you, Mr Rider. I'm sure that if there was anything—' she broke off, and glanced down at her clenched hands. 'As I said, Julia is not a criminal. A little high-spirited, perhaps, but she could have done nothing to warrant this persecution from this man. Whatever it is, I shall make it my business to clear everything up. This Mr Morven, and I don't care how many hotels he owns, is going to find out that he simply can't go around making trouble for my family. Not unless he wants to end up in the courts,' she added grimly, and at Mr Rider's raised eyebrows at her vehemence, she added quickly, 'Sorry, it's not your fight,' and walked to the door, then turned to face the manager. 'You see, I know my sister,' she said quietly before going back to her room to pack her belongings.

CHAPTER TWO

THIRTY minutes later, Edwina sat in a taxi on her way to the Haven. Her mind was seething with possibilities that might explain the events of the past, that had ended with her abrupt depature from the Splendour.

There was one possibility that had presented itself to her, and on the face of things seemed more than probable. Julia was a beauty who had turned many heads. It was not inconceivable that this Morven character had made advances to her and been well and truly repelled, and it was pure spite that had made him take his revenge on her sister.

That he had spotted the likeness between them was obvious, but Edwina had never been able to see the likeness. Julia's silver-fair hair and blue eyes bore no resemblance to her own strawberry blonde colouring, bordering, it was true, more on the blonde than on the red, but her eyes were nothing like Julia's. Edwina was tall, and stood at least seven inches above her sister's diminutive five feet height, and Edwina was hard put to it to work out how anyone could have recognised them as sisters, or even vaguely related.

What Edwina had failed to take into account were the mannerisms inherited from their parents. A certain way of holding one's head, a certain way of looking at people, even in some cases a similarity of voice, all little giveaways to the astute student of personalities.

Edwina leaned forward and steadied her large case as the taxi careered over the rutted road that led to the Haven. The more she thought about it, the more sure she was that she had the answer.

A man like that would not take too kindly to a rebuff. He was the type of man who always got what he wanted, that much was certain, and Julia was not a fool. She would lead a man on with shameless disregard for his feelings; she was so used to homage from all and sundry, she took their adoration for granted. Knowing Julia, Edwina surmised that she had found the Morven man a little harder to handle than her previous admirers, and liked her own way too much to be corralled into accepting his dictates. You couldn't play around with a man of that calibre, and Julia had done the only thing possible, run for it.

So certain was Edwina that she had the answer, she changed her directions to the taxi driver, asking him to take her to Kingfisher Bay, where Julia and Stanley's home was, perched up on top of a bluff overlooking the bay, after which the villa had been named. She might as well get confirmation from Julia while she was about it, then there would be a confab with Peter, who would advise her on how to proceed, for she was determined to bring the man to book. She had lost her job because of him, but worse than that, he had maligned the family name, and that Edwina simply was not going to allow!

As the taxi pulled into the long drive of King-fisher, Edwina debated about asking the driver to wait while she had a word with Julia, as the Haven was only a few miles away to the right of the bay, but she decided against this decision. Stanley would see that her case got delivered, and would probably run her back when she was ready to go, in any case some form of transport would be provided, so she paid off the driver after he had deposited her case on the porch of the villa.

Edwina found Julia in the sun lounge at the back of the villa, stretched out on a lilo enjoying the last warm rays of the sun before the sudden evening curtain fell.

'Good gracious!' Julia exclaimed at Edwina's entrance. 'Have you chucked the job up?' she enquired with a grin, as she sat up and reached for her wrap slung across a wicker chair next to her, and slipped it over her well tanned shoulders, the white of the wrap emphasising the tan.

'They've chucked me,' said Edwina, sitting down on the wicker chair. 'Ever heard of a man called Morven?' she asked casually, keeping a close watch on her sister.

Julia's start gave Edwina the confirmation that she sought—so she had been right, she thought.

'Of course I've heard of him,' said Julia, and reached for her cigarette case. 'He's a big noise, and he owned the hotel I worked for. Why?' she asked casually—too casually.

Edwina watched her light her cigarette with what looked like a very shaky movement. 'And that's all you know about him?' she persisted softly.

Julia gave a shrug that made the wrap slip off her shoulders, and as she retrieved it, her wide blue eyes looked at Edwina. 'What else?' she said airily.

Edwina knew that look well. The more candidly Julia looked at you, the more she had to hide, and Edwina absentmindedly wondered how long it would take Stanley to catch on. 'So there was something,' she said dryly. 'Okay, let's have it.'

Julia pouted. 'I don't see why that old thing should be dragged up,' she said complainingly, as she poured herself an iced drink from a beautiful cut glass jug on the table to her left. 'It's nothing to do with anyone else,' she added crossly.

'Oh, yes, it has,' Edwina replied firmly. 'I've just lost my job over it, whatever it was, so I think I've a right to know, don't you?'

Julia took a gulp of her drink, then shot Edwina a wary look. 'What's been said?' she asked.

Edwina sighed. This was not going to be easy, and she was glad she had sent the taxi away. Julia was playing for time, so whatever it was, it was serious, and Edwina felt the first pangs of uncertainty. 'Nothing,' Edwina said wearily. 'That's why I'm asking you. All I know is that at precisely three-thirty this afternoon, a Mr Morven walked into the Splendour, took one look at me, and went to Mr Rider's office. At precisely three-forty-five— zap! I'm out of a job—so you tell me.'

Julia gave an exaggerated sigh. 'I suppose he's bought the place?' she said, making it more of a statement than a question, and at Edwina's nod, went on, 'Look, this isn't something I want to get around. Stanley hasn't to hear about it.' She gave Edwina a pleading look. 'If he does hear about it, there'll be trouble, and really I'm not blaming Mr Morven—well, not really. I guess we were all a bit high. I certainly was, anyway,' she added, giving Edwina another of her wide-eyed looks.

'There was a party, you see,' Julia began slowly, her hesitancy telling Edwina that she was not liking telling the story, 'and Damon Morven—Oh, he'd thrown a few looks my way, and I knew he was interested, but when it's the boss—well, you have to watch your step. I'd heard a few things about him,' she shrugged. 'He hasn't much time for women—well, not permanently, that is. He's no monk, of course, and men like him can always get what they want.'

Edwina almost nodded her head in agreement. She had not misjudged the man, this description fitted with what she had seen of him.

'Well—' Julia went on, stubbing out her cigarette and immediately taking another, showing Edwina how nervous she was. Julia did not smoke that much as a rule. 'As I said, we were all at that party, all the staff, I mean. Mr Morven often gave them, it was his way of showing his appreciation to the staff,' she explained to the growingly impatient Edwina who wished she would get to the point. 'He's filthy rich,' Julia added, then gave a self-satisfactory smirk. 'I suppose Stanley's in the same bracket,' and she narrowed her eyes as she worked out the financial aspects, then at an impatient movement from Edwina, regretfully went back to the subject under discussion. 'There was lots of champagne,' she said, 'and I'm not used to it,' this was said in an almost complaining way, 'and I suppose that was why—' she hesitated, then went on quickly, 'the only thing I remember was waking up suddenly in Damon Morven's bed—so I took off, I was scared.' This last bit was added in a defiant tone that dared Edwina to probe further.

Edwina blinked and stared at Julia. She was shocked, and her voice showed it, as she asked incredulously, 'You mean you don't remember going into his bedroom?'

Julia gave an offhand shrug. 'I told you, I'd been drinking. We'd all been drinking.'

Edwina felt like shaking her head to remove the fog that had descended upon her. 'And Damon Morven?' she asked in a disbelieving tone. There was nothing she could put her finger on, but things did not sound right.

Julia stared at her cigarette. 'I didn't see him anywhere,' she said. 'I just woke up and realised where I was, and got out fast. I felt pretty awful, I can tell you,' she added fervently.

Edwina kept her eyes on Julia's face. 'How did you know it was his bedroom?' she asked quietly.

'Because the party was held in his apartment,' Julia replied irritably. 'And that's all there is to it. As I said, it's something I want to forget. If Stanley gets to hear about it, he'll take Damon Morven apart!' She gave Edwina another pleading look. 'It's not as if he was entirely to blame, is it? I'd had too much to drink, as I said, we were all a bit high, and I suppose I was flattered by his attentions, he's an attractive devil,' her voice trailed off as she listened for a moment, and Edwina heard the wheels of a car crunching on the drive. 'That's Stanley,' Julia said, and looked worried. 'Don't you dare say anything about this to him,' she warned Edwina.

Edwina got up slowly. There was still something that she couldn't put her finger on, a feeling that things didn't gell. 'So why did I have to get the sack?' she said in a low voice, although there was no chance of Stanley hearing them, since they could both see him unloading his fishing gear from the car outside the double garage opposite them.

Julia gave a long sigh. 'I guess he's still mad at me for running away,' she said. 'Girls don't walk out on him. He's the one to give the marching orders.'

Edwina felt immensely tired, and sad that Julia had not confided in her earlier. All this had taken place several months ago, and there had been ample opportunity for her to have told Edwina, and Edwina felt that she had failed her younger sister for not pressing for details as to why she had suddenly left her job.

It was all very well to be wise after the event, Edwina told herself sadly, as she sat in Stanley's car as he took her back to the Haven. Julia had not looked as if she had received the fright of her life when she had arrived back, just irritable – in fact, the same old Julia when bored with life.

One part of her listened idly to Stanley's enthusiastic account of his day's fishing, and the other part of her mind played with Julia's disclosures.

'I'm sure going to find it hard getting back into harness again,' Stanley commented, as he negotiated a particularly bad hole in the road. 'I'm due back in the States for a month or so,' he added.

Edwina came out of her musings and stared at him. 'I thought you were settled here,' she said in surprise.

Stanley gave a rueful grin. 'So I am,' he replied. 'But there's still business deals to be negotiated, and I have to be around for one rather important one. I've not said anything to Julia yet. I was hoping to duck out from under and let the staff get on with it, but I heard this morning that I have to be there. It'll mean spending at least a month in New York. Think Julia will mind?' he asked anxiously, 'I know she's pretty settled at the villa, but I'd want her with me.'

Edwina didn't need to think that one out. 'She'll love New York,' she assured Stanley. 'Julia loves change, you know. You've got no worries there,' she told him.

Particularly as Damon Morven had bought the Splendour, Edwina thought, and would undoubtedly be paying several visits to the island. Julia would be only too pleased to go to New York, or anywhere else for that matter, now that certain events had come to light. Her secret was safe with Edwina, but the very fact that Damon Morven had started operations on this island must have worried her.

Before he dropped her at the Haven, Stanley threw out an invitation for Edwina to accompany Julia to New York, saying that he would be tied up with business most of the time, and she would be company for Julia, but Edwina, although she was tempted to accept, refused the offer. As yet, Stanley did not know that she had lost her job at the Splendour, and Edwina had to look for another post, and she felt it was as well that Stanley and Julia should be off the scene during her job hunt, for she could always say that she had felt like a change when they came back and found her in another job.

Back at the Haven, Edwina went in search of Peter, but found that he was out on an evening fishing trip and wouldn't be back until late, so her news would have to keep until the following morning, which annoyed her, because she badly wanted to talk things over with him.

There was still that something that Edwina hadn't been able to put her finger on, and it continually nagged at the back of her consciousness, and after dinner she unpacked her case in the room that she had used before in the hotel, grateful for the fact that Peter's private quarters remained his own domain, in spite of the influx of guests at the height of the season.

It was such a beautiful evening, she decided not to sit about in her room, but went down to the beach where she could be sure of some peace, for the hotel bar was full of the fishing fraternity, talking, dreaming about the big one they would catch the next day, or the one that got away the previous day.

Out at sea the twinkling lights of the sea fishermen's boats glowed like little stars in the distance, bobbing up and down with the motion of the ocean. The soft breezes played on Edwina's hair as she gazed seawards, drinking in the peace around her, but unfortunately this sense of serenity did not last long, and she was back to her worries again.

The nagging little doubt that had teased her suddenly appeared in a clearer form, and at last she had it. Why had a man like Damon Morven still borne a grudge over something that had happened several months ago?

Was it possible that he had really fallen for Julia and was still intent on taking his revenge even though she was now beyond his reach? He must know that she had married Stanley Nelson. It had been in all the local gossip magazines, for the story was of interest, particularly because of the Rosewalls' earlier connection with the Islands.

Edwina sighed. It was the only answer that made sense to her, although just what he could have had to gain by such uncavalier treatment was beyond her, yet as she recalled her first impressions of the man, this solution appeared highly improbable. He was too hard to be taken in by Julia, in spite of her wide blue eyes, of this Edwina was certain.

A frown creased her smooth forehead. How could she be certain? Wasn't there a saying that went something like, 'the taller they were, the further they fell?' or something on those lines. It wasn't quite right, she knew, but it meant the same thing. Damon Morven was a big noise in his own world, and he wouldn't take too kindly to losing out. If he had fallen for Julia, and been rebuffed—she thought of Julia's words, 'When I woke up I found myself in his bed, and got out fast!'

Edwina swallowed: She didn't want to think about that part of it, she had deliberately pushed it to the back of her mind, but it had happened, and she was not inclined to be as forgiving as Julia had been, by her calm explanation that they had all been 'high'.

Had the man deliberately bought the Splendour in order to make trouble for Julia? Judging by his reaction to Edwina it certainly looked like it.

Edwina drew a deep breath. There was little chance of a cover-up where Stanley was concerned if this was so, and it might be better if they stayed on in New York for good. As for Stanley taking Damon Morven 'apart'—Edwina gave a wry grimace—Stanley would have to go into training for a very long period indeed if he contemplated any such action. Damon Morven's height alone, quite apart from his obvious fitness, against Stanley's short, rather rotund figure, would make it a one-sided contest.

Edwina shivered. It was not only the sea breezes that had got through to her, and she had the feeling that it would take more than a cardigan to warm her heart, because she was genuinely worried. Trust Julia to cause this amount of trouble, but it was her father's reaction that really worried her. He was a proud man, and his name held good in that part of the world, but if anything should cause a slur on his name—and it certainly would if this wretched man was out to make trouble for them, then—Edwina got up suddenly. It was no use getting into a stew, as friends were apt to remark kindly at times like this, 'it might never happen' and she was getting worked up for nothing. Tomorrow she would have a word with Peter, he would know what she should do about it, if there was anything that could be done, and at that moment in time Edwina could think of nothing, apart from spiking the man's guns by telling Stanley in confidence, and persuading him to take as broad a view of the happening as Julia herself had, and that would have to be Peter's job, she thought tiredly, as she went back into the hotel and prepared for bed.

CHAPTER THREE

EDWINA had left a note for Peter to find when he got back from the fishing trip, telling him that she was back, and would see him in the morning, and when she walked into his small dining room the following morning he had already ordered breakfast for her.

In spite of her worries, she had slept well, and she thought it must have been the evening air that had helped her to have a good night, and her reply to Peter's chirpy 'good morning' to her was almost as cheery, for it was hard to be downcast on such a lovely morning, and things always seemed brighter in the morning.

She was soon to lose her restored spirits, for Peter's reaction to the news she was to give him brought back her worries.

'Decided to have a few days off?' was his opening remark, as Edwina sat down at the table.

'Not exactly,' she replied carefully, wondering how to start on her narration. 'There's a new boss at the Splendour, and he took exception to my presence.'

Peter raised an eyebrow. 'How come?' he asked, as he handed her the butter for her bread roll. 'What's he got against you?'

'Against me personally, nothing,' Edwina replied, 'it appears to be the family he's got it in for.'

Peter, about to take a bite of a piece of toast, held it suspended in mid-air, and frowned. 'In that case you'd better tell me all,' he said. 'I'm in it too, aren't I?'

'Do you know a man named Damon Morven?' asked Edwina—and received much the same reaction as she had had from Julia.

'Of course I know him,' Peter replied frowningly. 'I shouldn't think there's anybody that lives out here that hasn't heard of him. He owns several hotels round and about—' He stopped. 'Has he bought the Splendour?' he asked suddenly, and at Edwina's swift nod, gave a nod himself. 'I'm not surprised, he's been waiting for a foothold over here for some time.' He looked at Edwina. 'You mean he's the one—?'

Edwina nodded again. 'He also owns the hotel Julia worked for,' she nodded meaningly, although Peter did not get the connection.

'Well?' he asked Edwina. 'What's he got to do with it?'

'Everything,' she replied sourly, and launched into the story, hesitating only when it came to the reason for Julia's flight from the island.

Peter still hadn't got the connection, and it was Edwina's fault, for all she had said was that Julia had got tipsy at a party and had to get out fast.

'I still don't see—' he began.

'Oh, come on!' Edwina exploded. 'You're not half as dense as you make out. Julia had too much to drink at a party at the hotel, and—well, she came to,' she gritted her teeth, 'in Damon Morven's bed,' she ended limply.

Peter's brown eyes blinked behind his horn-rimmed spectacles; there was no vagueness in his expression now. 'Silly little devil!' he exclaimed furiously. 'That's one of the oldest tricks in the game. I might have known she'd try something like that, and no wonder she had to leave in a hurry,' he added sourly.

It was Edwina's turn to stare. 'What do you mean by "trying it on"?' she demanded indignantly. 'If anyone was trying it on, it was this man Morven. She was drunk, I tell you!'

Peter gave a derisive snort. 'That girl could drink me under the table,' he said, 'and if she'd come to me with that story, I'd have told her to pull the other leg.' He gave Edwina a sympathetic look. 'She could always hoodwink you, couldn't she? As for Damon Morven taking advantage of her,' he gave another derisive snort, 'you'd have to be up early to do that with a girl like Julia. You can take my word for it that nothing would have happened to her, apart from hearing a few well chosen remarks that must have hurt her pride somewhat. Morven's not such a fool as to fall for a trick like that. You don't think she's the only one that's tried a dodge like that, do you? I should think he's got the routine down to a T by now.' He nodded to himself. 'He probably told her to get off the island pronto, probably gave her a deadline—and serve her right, little fool!' he added feelingly.

He glanced at the shocked Edwina, who was

finding it hard to believe what Peter had said. 'Look, it's no use beating about the bush, Edwina. If you don't know Julia by now, you'll never know her. She's been spoilt for years. Even I fell for those baby blue eyes of hers years ago—to be honest, she was the reason why I made so many trips home in the last few years—but after standing on the side-lines and doing a little birdwatching, It didn't take me long to see that that gorgeous façade of hers *was* only a façade. Underneath, she's a grasping opportunist. She played the field back home, didn't she? How many boy-friends have you lost to her?' he asked Edwina gently. 'Only being you, you stood by and let her make hay. I'm damn glad she met her match in Morven, I only wish I could have been there to witness it,' he gave a sudden grin as he pictured the scene.

Edwina looked away from the amusement in Peter's face. It was all very well for him, she thought angrily. He hadn't lost his job through Julia's actions, or his good name. Deep down Edwina knew that she couldn't challenge Peter's findings, because she was sure that he was right. Julia had lied to her, as she had done on so many other occasions when it suited her. Either way, she thought dully, it couldn't be proved.

That, she thought, settled it. The chances of her finding other employment on the island were very slight indeed. She could work for Peter, for he would offer if she asked, she knew, but sooner or later she would run up against Damon Morven, and the thought of facing him with what she now knew was something she was not prepared to do, so it was home for her. Julia would have to fight her own battles for a change, and no doubt win, as she had in the past.

'I'm going home,' she said abruptly, pushing her half eaten breakfast away from her with a decisive action.

Peter stared at her. 'I thought you'd settled down here?' He said in surprise, and pointed an accusing finger at her. 'If you're letting Julia's exploits ruin everything for you, then go, but it's time you started living your own life. She's married now, and no concern of yours. It's her husband's worry now, and he's no fool, he'll keep her in line, you'll see.'

Edwina was not convinced. 'The trouble is,' she pointed out quietly, 'I still have the name of Rosewall, and the man knows we're sisters. I can only thank goodness that Father will never get to hear of it.' Her lovely tawny eyes narrowed in thought. 'What do you think he'd have done about it, if he'd been here?' she asked Peter.

He shrugged. 'Dragged her by the scruff of the neck to see Morven and made her apologise to him,' he replied. 'He hasn't got rose-tinted spectacles where Julia's concerned either,' he added meaningly.

Edwina gave a slow nod in agreement. That was exactly what her father would have done. As it was, she was helpless.

Peter watched her expression, and rightly judged her thoughts. 'If you're so worried about the slur on your name, and I don't think you've any need to be—after all, it's many years since your father worked out here, and many people will have forgotten the connection—' he shrugged, 'you could always go and apologise for her.'

Edwina gave him an ironical look. He had conveniently forgotten the write-up in the local magazines about the wedding a few months ago. If anyone had forgotten the connection of the name of Rosewall with the Islands, then that piece of gossip would have reminded them. 'No, thank you,' she said tartly, and added vehemently, 'Look, nothing's been proved, has it? For once, Julia could have been telling the truth, couldn't she? And if you think I'm going on my knees to that man, when I'm not totally convinced that he's not to blame for what happened, then you can think again,' she added crossly.

Peter gave an exaggerated sigh. 'Go and face her with it, then,' he said patiently. 'If you still think she's innocent, then you'll make all kinds of trouble for yourself in trying to prove it, and I think you know that. Julia is poison—and I'm not apologising for that remark. You'd have been happily married to that dentist chap of yours wouldn't you, by now, if she hadn't spiked your guns. It's time you faced up to a few facts about your little sister, unpalatable as they are.'

There was silence while Edwina digested this. She hadn't thought of Philip for months. It was a part of her life that she had refused to acknowledge. It also served to remind her that if she went home, she would not be able to stay at home. She did not want that association renewed.

'Well?' asked Peter. 'Are you going to let her drive you away? Or are you going to do something about it?'

Edwina squared her shoulders. 'No,' she said abruptly. 'I shall see her, and get it straightened out.' She looked at Peter. 'If you're right about what happened,' she swallowed, 'then I shall go to see the man, and apologise on behalf of the family. And it won't be easy for me. I heartily disliked what I saw of him, but I shall do it,' she added with gritted teeth.

Peter nodded complacently. 'That's the stuff,' he said. 'At least he'll know you're not tarred with the same brush. He's a hard man, but a fair one, businesswise, anyway. You can't blame him for his attitude towards women either. I guess there's enough fortune-hunters around these islands to make up three pirate ships, and they're all females on the lookout for rich husbands,' he added with a grin, 'but they've got their work cut out with Morven. He's a buccaneer of a special kind.'

After breakfast, Edwina begged transport from Peter, who readily agreed to take her to King-fisher's Bay, saying that he had a date with Stanley anyway, and was taking him out beyond the reefs, and that it would be an all-day excursion, which was perfect for Edwina's purpose. She only hoped that Julia had not arranged to entertain another 'fishing widow' for the day, but she would have to take her chance on that.

Julia had, but happily for Edwina it was only for a

coffee morning, and that left the two girls with the afternoon to themselves.

Julia, by now, knew of the coming trip to New York, and the morning was spent on her enthusing remarks on the coming trip, while a Mrs Sawton, the wife of a business friend of Stanley's, regaled her with all the sights she must see, and what to avoid. As a New Yorker herself, she was well qualified to give advice, and provided Julia with a list of her acquaintances to get in touch with, ending with, 'Gee, I wish I were going with you! I guess I'm missing city life. If I hear one more fishing story from Larry—'

Mrs Sawton left shortly after midday, and Julia and Edwina settled down to a lazy afternoon on the loggia after a light lunch.

Edwina knew that Julia was aware that there had to be a reason for her visit, and judging by the way she would fill in any slight uncomfortable pause with little mundane remarks such as doing as Mrs Sawton had suggested and waiting until she got to New York before buying any clothes, as the island's stock was a trifle limited, etc., she had a good idea on the subject Edwina wanted to discuss.

'About Damon Morven,' Edwina began firmly, deciding there was nothing for it but to go right in at the deep end.

'What about him?' Julia cut in swiftly. 'I told you what happened, and I don't want to discuss it.'

'I'm afraid you're going to have to,' Edwina replied grimly. 'I don't think you told me as much as you could have done.' She did not say that Julia had lied to her, but the implication was there.

Julia's soft lips pouted sullenly. 'Want the sordid details, do you?' she asked angrily.

Edwina's brows lifted. 'Of course not, and that's not what I meant,' she replied, now as angry as Julia. 'Look, by what you told me, that man got you drunk and—well, we won't go into that, but look at it from my point of view. Do you think I'm going to let him get away with it—or Stanley, come to that? Of course I'm not! If I can't get the truth from you then I'm going to see him and get it straightened out. One way or another, I'm going to hear the whole of it,' she added threateningly.

Julia got up from her lilo and walked to the door, and Edwina thought she was going to walk out on her, until she heard her call for Jasmine, her young island servant girl who lived in on the premises, and waited on the family, to bring some iced drinks to the loggia, then she slowly walked back to join Edwina. She's playing for time, Edwina thought, but it wasn't going to get her anywhere, she thought grimly.

After the drinks had been brought, and the smiling lithe girl had glided away to her other duties in the villa, Julia poured herself out a drink, leaving Edwina to get her own, and as this was typical of Julia, Edwina did not take exception but got herself a drink. Julia, it appeared, was fighting a losing battle with her conscience, and Edwina had no doubt that her threat to go and see Damon Morven had brought about this dilemma.

Without realising it, Julia carried out the conversation she was having in her mind. 'Oh, he'd enjoy telling that,' she got out between clenched teeth. She gave Edwina a startled look, as she realised what she'd just said, then gave a shrug. 'What the hell!' she said resignedly. 'All right, if you want the truth you can have it. You won't be paying any visits to Damon Morven, though, not unless you want to be made to feel as if you were a tramp, because that's how he made me feel.

'Do you know what it feels like when someone looks right through you?' she demanded of Edwina. 'Well, that's how he treated me—me!' she emphasised furiously. 'And he had the effrontery to warn me against flirting with the guests—as if I could stop those stupid men hanging around!' She drew in a deep breath. 'So I thought I'd teach him a lesson.' She shrugged. 'As I said, there was a party and I got a little high. I sneaked into his room and waited for him in his bed. I wanted to see just how cool and uninterested he'd be after that!'

Edwina's heart sank. It was one thing to suspect, but quite another to be certain. She had known that Peter's interpretation of what had happened was probably right, but it had not stopped her from hoping that he was wrong.

It was so typical of Julia, so used to adoration from all and sundry, she just hadn't been able to believe that there was a man who could resist her charms. So wrapped up in herself was she that she would never consider the consequences of such an action.

'You said you woke up in his bed,' she reminded Julia remorselessly. She had to hear the whole of it now that so much of it had been told, she didn't want to, but she had to.

Julia gave her a smouldering look. 'Oh, I'd have gone through with it if he'd—' she gave Edwina an irritated look. 'Why shouldn't I? What's it to you? You always were such a prude,' she added angrily.

Edwina chose to ignore that last bit. 'So you didn't spend the night there?' she persisted doggedly.

'I didn't spend ten minutes there, if you must know!' Julia almost shouted at her. 'He was absolutely furious. I told you I was scared, and I damn well was. He gave me precisely one hour to get out of the hotel, bag and baggage. And believe me, I couldn't get out fast enough!'

Edwina said nothing. There was nothing she could say.

'Go on,' Julia taunted her furiously, 'read me the lecture about nice girls not doing things like that!'

Edwina just sighed, and stared down into her drink. 'It's a bit too late for that, isn't it?' she said gently, 'and I suppose you must have had a rotten time afterwards.' She looked at her sister, who was now looking down at her slim sandalled feet. One blonde curl had fallen forward on to her forehead and made her look somehow defenceless.

This gentle rebuke produced a reaction that Edwina had never seen in Julia before, because she burst out crying, and in between sobs told Edwina of her fear that Stanley might get to hear of it. 'I know he doesn't cut a very romantic figure, but I do care for him,' she got out tearfully. 'I've never felt safe with anybody before, but if anything should happen to him, I don't know what I'd do. You don't know what it's like,' she told Edwina, twisting her fine lawn handkerchief in her hands. 'You thought I was only playing about with Philip, didn't you? Well, I wasn't, I really thought I was in love with him.'

She blew her nose and gave a loud sniff. 'Do you know what happened after you broke off the engagement?' Her reddened eyes stared at Edwina. 'He dropped me flat. Said it was my fault that you were through with him, and that he'd been a damn fool.'

She swallowed. 'That's what they're all like. I'm tired of being chased by men who only want a good time. They don't settle for my type, we're only good for a bit on the side.' She blew her nose again. 'But Stanley's not like that. He's honest and true, and he really loves me, and I'm sure I love him. Oh, not in the passionate wild way that they talk about in novels, but in a sort of comfortable, sure way.' She glanced at Edwina. 'I'm so worried about what that man might do or say to hurt Stanley. I didn't think I'd hear any more about it, but after what happened to you, I've been worried sick inside,' she confided. 'I know I ought to tell Stanley, but somehow I can't. I've even considered getting him to move off the island, especially now that that man has bought that hotel,' she added woefully.

Edwina thought of what Peter had said her father

would do, and it might work, she thought, for she could well understand Julia's reluctance to tell her husband, although she doubted if it would make any difference to them, for Stanley was absolutely besotted with Julia, still—'How about going to see Mr Morven and apologising to him?' she suggested quietly. 'They say he's a fair man,' she added coaxingly.

Julia shuddered. 'No, thank you!' she said abruptly, giving the same reaction that Edwina herself had given to Peter when he had suggested such a course of action. 'I absolutely couldn't! I doubt if I'd get past reception, anyway.' She looked hopefully at Edwina. 'Couldn't you have a word with him? Tell him I was drunk—tell him anything, just as long as he leaves us alone,' she pleaded.

This placed Edwina on the spot, for in spite of her brave assertion to Peter on what she would do if she found out that Julia was guilty, she had since had second thoughts and decided to do no such thing. It was highly improbable that she would get past reception either, come to that.

Her doubtful glance rested on Julia's tear-stained face, and before she realised what she was saying, she had said, 'Well, I can only try,' after which Julia's relief and absolute certainty that everything would be all right, made it impossible for Edwina to back out.

Edwina left her sister at four o'clock, deciding not to wait for the return of Peter and Stanley, and transport back to the Haven, and walked the mile back to the hotel.

She had a lot to think about, and how to approach the problem Julia had landed her with, castigating herself for being such a weak-kneed fool as to make the offer, or allow Julia to put her in the spot she was in.

Several times she almost turned around to make her way back to the villa to tell Julia that she simply couldn't go through with it, but the thought of her father kept her marching forward.

It didn't matter what he said to her—if she did get to speak to him, that was; the main thing was that she would have attempted to make the apology, and that was the right thing to do. Nothing else mattered.

By the time she reached the hotel, she had still not made up her mind how to approach Damon Morven. Whether to ring up and make an appointment to see him, or whether to just turn up at the Splendour and ask to see him, if he was there, of course, neither of which she fancied, but coward-like, she preferred to make a call to the Splendour. If he refused to see her, then she would have tried, and that would be an end to it.

As she neared the front of the hotel, a taxi drew up in the courtyard and deposited an elderly man and his baggage at the hotel, and suddenly Edwina's mind was made up. As soon as the driver had carried the man's luggage into the hotel foyer, Edwina asked him to take her to the Splendour.

Her breath was coming in uneven gasps as she sat back in the taxi and tried to quell her agitation. Why on earth had she acted on the spur of the moment like that? She hadn't even talked it over with Peter, and here she was on her way to what could be a very unpleasant interview indeed.

A tiny voice inside her whispered that the sooner it was over the better, and Edwina drew a deep sigh. It was that thought that had propelled her forward. She didn't want it hanging over her head, and it had to be done.

Suddenly she was calm again, and impatient to get to the Splendour, and when the taxi swept into the wide frontage of the hotel and drew up, she was out, and paying the driver, as if she had a train to catch.

The collywobbles struck again as she walked into the reception area, for it suddenly occurred to her that the girls at reception might know why she had been dismissed, and she felt a sick sensation at the pit of her stomach, then taking a deep breath she approached the desk, but before she reached it a voice pulled her up in her tracks.

'Forgot something, did you, Miss Rosewall?'

Edwina did not need to turn round to identify that voice, she had only heard it once before, but it had made an impression on her, not to mention the following sequences, she thought dourly, as she turned to face Damon Morven. 'I wanted a word with you,' she said, keeping her voice low, and she hoped on an even keel, but she was shaking inside, and hating the position she was in.

For a blessed moment she thought he was going to show her the door, and she was only too willing to oblige him, but as if a thought had occurred to him, he lifted his dark brows in an almost satirical fashion. 'Do you, now? I wonder why?'

Edwina felt the heat rise in her cheeks. She had known it was not going to be easy, but how could you apologise to a man like this? she thought. A man who took pleasure out of someone's discomfiture. 'I wish to make an apology on behalf of my sister,' she said stiffly, and would have gone on if he had not stopped her.

'I don't think the hotel reception is the place for this kind of conversation, do you?' he said silkily, then in an abrupt tone, ordered, 'Follow me,' and Edwina was obliged to follow in his tall wake to a room off reception that had been made into an office. It had once been a small lounge where the office staff had had their breaks, but now the easy chairs had been pushed aside for a large imposing desk and various items of office furniture.

Once inside, Edwina purposely left the door open, for obvious reasons. She did not like or trust this man, and if he thought she was going to provide him with some amusing entertainment, then he was going to be disappointed!

'Please close the door, Miss Rosewall,' he commanded, politely—too politely, for it smacked of sarcasm. 'I don't usually ravish women until after eight in the evening, a fact that your sister didn't take into consideration,' he added sneeringly.

Edwina flushed to the roots of her hair, but instead of closing the door she began to walk towards it. She was not putting up with this. Julia would have to do her own apologising.

'Oh, for heaven's sake, woman! Sit down!' he
barked at her. 'You came to make an apology.
Okay, go ahead,' he ordered, settling down in the
chair behind the desk, which had the effect of
making the whole thing an inquisition.

Edwina stiffened and turned back slowly, then
took the chair opposite the desk. 'There's nothing
much more to be said,' she said stiffly. 'Julia ought
to have come herself,' her lovely eyes dropped
from his sceptical grey gaze, 'but under the circumstances—' she swallowed, then looked up
directly at him. 'You know she's married now?' she
asked; she was sure that he did, but he gave no sign,
she carried on bravely. 'Well, obviously it's embarrassing for her,' she ended lamely.

'So it worked with some poor devil, did it?' he
sneered. 'He has my profound sympathy.'

Edwina gasped, as the full impact of what he was
hinting swept over her. Peter had said that it was
the oldest trick in the game—and he thought
Julia—she clenched her hands to stop them trembling. 'Julia was—' she swallowed, but made herself go on; somehow she had to make this hateful
man understand. 'Julia had had too much to drink,'
she said, willing herself not to shout at him. 'She
could hardly be responsible for her actions.'

'She wasn't too drunk to know which was my
bedroom,' Damon Morven said sarcastically.
'There were only eighteen on that floor to chose
from.'

Edwina's eyes showed their consternation. So
the party hadn't been held in his apartment. Julia

had still lied to her. She got up swiftly, there was absolutely no point in carrying on the conversation. She had apologised, and that was that. 'Well, I have apologised,' she said between clenched teeth. It cost her a lot to repeat that apology, but she had done it, and the sooner she was out of this detestable man's vicinity, the happier she would be.

'Just a minute, Miss Rosewall,' the smooth insolent voice reached her as she got to the door. 'Aren't you going to ask for your job back? That's really why you've come, isn't it?'

Edwina's hands clenched by her side. 'As a matter of fact, it wasn't,' she got out coldly. 'I felt an apology was due to you, and I've given it, but I see that I needn't have bothered. Good afternoon, Mr Morven. I sincerely hope we shall not meet again!'

This should have been her grand exit line, but it fell rather flat, as to her annoyance, Damon Morven got to the door first, moving with incredible speed for a man of his size, and made Edwina come to an abrupt halt in front of the door.

To her further fury it appeared that he was not prepared to let her have the last word. His cold grey eyes went slowly over her firm contours, for Edwina was no fragile flower. 'Why don't you ask for your job back?' he taunted her. 'There's no need to stand on your dignity. I might agree to take you on again. Mr Rider was most put out when you left. I understand you are a good worker.'

Edwina almost shuddered at the purring inflection in his voice. She had not liked the way his cold eyes had roamed her figure either, or the way they were now searing into hers, as if willing her to do as he asked. 'No, thank you,' she said icily, her dislike of the man making her take a step back from him, and which he countermanded by taking a step towards her, to her added fury.

'I find women so often say "no" when they mean "yes",' he said softly, and to Edwina's consternation, reached up to touch her cheek with a lean finger. 'Now if it had been you I'd discovered that evening,' his finger went lightly down her cheek, 'things might have been different,' he added silkily, then his hand dropped abruptly away from her. 'I've an idea you'd give me a run for my money.' His voice was hard as he stepped back away from the door, indicating that Edwina was free to go. 'All you have to do is lift the telephone, but don't take too long about it. I lose interest pretty quickly,' he advised her stonily.

Edwina did not remember leaving the office, but she must have done, for when her panic-stricken senses calmed down she was in a taxi heading for the Haven.

The only thing that had brought a sense of sanity about the whole nightmarish episode was that low harsh chuckle of his as she flew through the office door on feet that seemed to have gained wings, so great was her agitation.

Now, as her heartbeats steadied, she recalled that laugh, and called herself all kinds of a fool for panicking the way she had.

Damon Morven had had his entertainment for the day, and she had unwittingly provided it. He had enjoyed frightening her, and he'd certainly succeeded! She shivered, in spite of the warm early evening air, and the closeness in the taxi.

She wouldn't trust that man under handcuffed conditions! What a fool Julia had been in thinking she could handle him with her foolish wiles. Knowing the kind of man he was, Edwina found herself surprised that he hadn't taken advantage of the situation, and thrown Julia out afterwards. It would only have been her word against his, and Julia would have come off a poor second in any action taken to redress the balance.

The nails of her fingers dug into the softness of her palms, but she felt no pain. What a fool she had been in thinking that he would have accepted an apology! It would have been far better if she had left things as they were.

Her well-meant action had only culminated in making her feel cheap. She shivered again. Had that man really expected her to accept his dubious offer? All she had to do, he'd said, was to lift the telephone, and as for that remark about not being too long about it or he'd lose interest—she shook her head bewilderedly. She had actually heard him say that, but she couldn't believe it. Men did not say things like that to women they hardly knew, did they?

She swallowed. Men did say things like that to girls who were on the make, and that was precisely what he thought about her. He was sure that her only purpose in going to see him was to get her job back. Julia's stupidity had tarred her with the same brush. His sneering comments on her marriage had proved that, and with what Peter had said about it being one of the oldest tricks in the game, it was not surprising that he should take that attitude.

Edwina's eyes closed as a thought suddenly struck her that he had not known about Julia's marriage. She had not been certain about this before, but she was now. He would hardly have called Stanley a 'poor devil', would he? She drew in a quick breath. He could not have been in the Bahamas at the time of the wedding, or even for a month or two afterwards. Even someone as wrapped up in business as Peter had hinted he was could have failed to either hear or read about the marriage.

It was beginning to look as if it would be better if Julia did manage to persuade Stanley to stay in New York, or maybe move to Bermuda, anywhere in fact, than stay where they were. Either that, or Julia would have to come clean and confess all to Stanley, and at least prepare him for what might happen should they meet up with the wretched man in the future.

Edwina could well imagine how such a meeting would go, with Damon Morven openly offering his profound condolences to Stanley! She swallowed. It would be simply awful! And although Julia had got herself into the mess, she hardly deserved to pay as much as that for it. Why, she might even lose Stanley! Edwina sat up straight as this thought occurred to her. Of course she wouldn't lose Stanley. He loved her—adored her, in fact, but there was no doubt that his pride would be in for a bad jolt.

The taxi drew up in front of the Haven's reception area, and Edwina saw with a rush of relief that Peter's car was outside his office, so she paid off the taxi driver and went in search of him.

Peter was having a word with Miss Toomy, the receptionist, when Edwina walked into reception, and after taking one look at her, for the shock she had received from Damon Morven still lingered in her lovely amber eyes, Peter quickly ended the conversation he was having with his receptionist and went to meet Edwina. 'You look as if you could do with a drink,' he said. 'Come on, we'll go to the lounge,' and he led the way to his private quarters.

Edwina, accepting the small brandy Peter had given her, took a slow sip of it before settling in one of the easy chairs, and gave Peter a wry smile. 'It shows, does it?' she said dryly.

Peter nodded. 'Bad, was it?' he asked, as he carried his whisky and soda to a chair opposite her and sat down, then leant forward in a conspiratorial fashion. 'He was not, I gather, in a very good mood?' he asked, his brows raising in an almost comical expression.

Edwina stared at him, then blinked. 'How did you know I'd seen him?' she asked. 'I presume we're both talking about Damon Morven?' she queried.

Peter grinned. 'I had a few minutes' talk with Julia while Stanley was cleaning up his fishing gear,' and at Edwina's accusing look at him, he shook his head. 'No, I didn't say anything. She brought the subject up herself. Wanted to know if I knew.' He shrugged. 'There was no point in saying I didn't. I'd have had to know eventually, wouldn't I? If only to explain what happened to you. She wouldn't, of course, have seen that side of it. Julia's only thought is for Julia,' he added sourly. 'Anyway, I gathered that you'd offered to go and see him for her. I'm afraid I did go for her then. Told her she should have gone herself, and that she should think about it. When I got back and found that you weren't around, then I guessed where you'd gone. She even,' Peter added indignantly, 'tried to get me involved, and suggested that I have a word with Morven, in case you backed out.'

Edwina's glance fell on her glass and at her fingers curled tightly around the stem. 'It might have been better at that,' she said, in a low voice. 'At least he wouldn't have made you feel like a streetwalker,' she added vehemently.

Peter's brows rose at this, and his brown eyes blinked owlishly behind his spectacles. 'I say, bad as that, was it? Damn Julia!' he got out between clenched teeth. 'So there was more to it than just a silly prank. Not that you'd get the whole truth from her. It was a try-on all right, just as I'd thought it was.'

Edwina gave him a surprised look. 'Oh, no, Peter. It was just Julia's way of paying him back for telling her off for flirting with the guests. You know Julia. She can't bear being treated like other people. She's been so spoilt she thinks she's special.'

Peter gave her a pitying look. 'You're hanging on to illusions again, aren't you?' he said. 'Look, there are some men who still have old-fashioned ideas, in spite of this day and age. Julia's got a good background, and it might have worked if it had been anyone else but Damon Morven. Men like him don't get drunk, so it didn't come off. Stanley, now, is in a different category. He's one of the old-fashioned types and doesn't play around with women.' His lips thinned. 'He's too nice a guy to be hurt, but he's in for a shock, I'm afraid.'

Edwina drew in a quick breath. 'But he doesn't have to be told, does he? I mean, if Julia can think up some reason for leaving the Out-Islands, then everything will be all right, won't it?' she asked anxiously.

Peter gave her another pitying look. 'Morven's enterprises are not confined to the Out-Islands,' he said dryly. 'He's interests all over the place, Bermuda, America—you name it. He's a big fish, Edwina. That was the only thing our Julia did get right. Now that he's got the Splendour, there's no doubt he'll be after more territory here.' He frowned. 'There's a fight going on at the moment between two big consortiums for a marina that's due to be built a few miles from here, and I wouldn't be surprised if he was one of the contestants, and if he is, Martin Canfourth might as well go fly a kite in the Hebrides, for all the chance he's got of landing it,' he mused thoughtfully, entirely losing track of Edwina's problem.

Edwina simply was not interested in the marina, or who got it. She had more pressing matters to attend to. She thought of Julia's suggestion of Peter acting as peacemaker, and it looked as if that was the only hope. If he could just explain about Julia, tell him she wasn't really a fortune-hunter— 'Couldn't you go and see Damon Morven?' she asked suddenly. 'At least he won't try and proposition you,' she added sardonically.

Peter gave her a startled look. 'I'd rather not,' he said hastily. 'I gather he doesn't know we're related, and I'd want to keep things that way,' and at Edwina's look of indignation, he went on, 'Look, Edwina, I'm in business here. I don't particularly want to get on the wrong side of a man like that. Chances are he'll get that marina, and although I'm doing very nicely, thank you, at the moment, I couldn't guarantee it continuing if a certain person took exception to my presence here.'

Edwina's chin went up and she sent Peter a half scathing and half accusing look, that showed what she thought of his excuses—in a word, cowardice!

Peter sighed. 'See it from my point of view, Edwina,' he said irritably. 'You see that part of the beach at the end of the hotel drive, the one that we launch our boats from?' he indicated the area with an outstretched arm, 'Well, whoever gets that marina also gets all the coastline this end of the island. With goodwill, I can keep it. Without it, I may as well go and join Martin in the Hebrides,' he added gloomily.

Edwina stared at him aghast. 'But I thought you owned the hotel,' she said.

Peter shrugged. 'So I do, but only the hotel, not the beach area. I had nothing to worry about, until there was this talk about the marina, and if it's being built on Star Point, and I'm certain it will be, then this strip of the beach is bound to be included. As I said, with a little goodwill I could continue to use it, maybe become part of the marina for the deep sea fishing enthusiasts,' he sighed. 'If Martin got it, I'd have no worries, but as things stand, it would be pointless if I went and antagonised the man who most probably will get it.'

Edwina felt depressed. Julia's foolishness was going to have a few more backlashes before it was over. Julia never did anything by half, she mused gloomily, then she sat up straight as an idea presented itself. 'Why don't you get Stanley to buy the marina?' she asked brightly. 'That would solve all our problems, wouldn't it?' adding as another thought struck her, 'Morven doesn't know he's married Julia, you see. Incredibly, he appears to have been off the scene at that time.'

It was Peter's turn to give Edwina an accusing look. 'You mean try a subtle kind of blackmail, do you?' he queried with a hint of indignation in his voice. 'Because his wife's a fool? Can you imagine the kind of mud-slinging that would start once Morven catches on as to who his wife is?' he asked pithily. 'Even if it was on—and it's not—I happen to know that Stanley's interests lie in oil, and only oil. His whole reason for settling here was to give himself a break from business ulcers. The only one who would enjoy the infighting would be Julia, and I'm damned if I'm going to give her that satisfaction. I've got too much regard for Stanley to push that angle,' he added adamantly.

Edwina nodded, and gave a long sigh. 'I'm sorry, Peter,' she said contritely. 'I suppose I'm not thinking straight.'

Peter patted her arm in an understanding action. 'Another brandy?' he suggested with a wry grin. 'We haven't lost all yet,' he reminded her in an attempt at levity.

Edwina shook her head. 'I'd rather not,' she replied, as she watched Peter go and refill his glass. A day ago, she had not heard of a man called Morven, now it seemed her whole future was in jeopardy because of him. No, correction, because of Julia, for Julia had tangled with the man, and here was Peter, who, if his assumptions were right, was also going to have his future jeopardised by the same pestilential man. 'That Martin somebody you mentioned,' she said, turning her thoughts to Peter's worries. 'Hasn't he got any chance of getting the marina?' she asked.

Peter took a sip from his glass. 'It all depends on the opposition,' he said. 'If Morven's in the running, then I'd say, no hope. If it's some other company, then maybe,' he shrugged. 'He's got the conservationists on his side, and that's a help, but where big money is concerned—' He gave another shrug.

Edwina frowned. 'How does conservation come into it?' she asked.

'There's a lot of folk who don't like the idea of turning the place into a glorified holiday camp, which is what it will become if the wrong company gets the land. Oh, it will be called a marina because plans have been passed for such an amenity, but if it's in the wrong hands, it won't be what you and I and a few others think of as a marina. There'll be a huge complex built, that will include shopping facilities, and a casino—all the amenities, in fact, that can be got on any other island but this one. That's why we're special, and wish to remain so. So far,' he added grimly, 'we've held our own and no one's made a serious bid to alter things, although there have been rumours.'

He stared gloomily into his glass. 'Martin booked in this morning. He's been coming here for years, but he usually chooses a quieter time, and the very fact that he's here means that there's something brewing, and things are hotting up. They're holding a meeting in the hotel this evening. It all depends on Colonel Melway, who appears to be dithering between the two warring sides. He's enough influence to swing the deal Martin's way, but if it is Morven he would have done his homework on the Colonel's weaknesses, unfortunately he likes a flutter at the tables, but he can't have it both ways. Either this part of the island remains exclusively for the fishing fraternity, or it joins the rest of the tourist circus.'

Edwina was beginning to see what Peter meant

about things not being too hopeful, and sighed inwardly. No wonder Peter wanted to stay clear of Damon Morven, just in case it was his company that was making a bid for the marina.

Edwina got up as the dinner gong resounded through the hotel. She knew that Peter would make the rounds of the tables to ensure himself that everything was going smoothly and that his guests were receiving the attention they paid so well for, and would not have his meal until after the guests had been fed, and although a table would be reserved for her in the dining room, she preferred to have her meal with Peter in the privacy of his quarters, and that gave her plenty of time to go to her room and freshen up before the meal.

'Why not come to the meeting?' Peter asked her, before they parted at the door of the lounge.' We could use somebody to take notes. If we do get the Colonel to give his blessing, we'll have it down in black and white and he won't be able to renege on us later,' he added with a grin. 'That's if you're interested?' he queried. 'I gather you'd rather be with the opposition?'

Edwina did not need any time to think that one over. 'If it's Damon Morven you're up against, I'm with you to the bitter end,' she said, with a fervency that made Peter's grin widen, before he gave a pleased nod and went to join the diners.

CHAPTER FOUR

DURING dinner, Peter filled Edwina in on who would be at the meeting. 'I think it would be better if I introduced you as my secretary,' he said apologetically. 'I don't want the opposition to get hold of any juicy titbits at this point in the negotiations,' he explained with a rueful grin.

Edwina agreed. She understood perfectly, and she felt like an undercover agent, but it was in a good cause and no harm would be done if Damon Morven was not involved. In any case, she was happy to have something to do to help, she had no job now, and plenty of time on her hands.

The meeting was held in Peter's lounge later that evening, and as roomy as the lounge was, it soon filled up as the time of the meeting approached.

Several chairs had been commissioned from the dining room, and the more prominent members were steered to easy chairs at the front of the gathering, with Edwina sitting tucked away against a wall at a bureau with notebook and pen at the ready, and looking very businesslike.

Just before the meeting began, Peter drew everyone's attention to Edwina, explaining that he thought it might be a good idea if his secretary took a few notes during the meeting, and which received the hearty approval of all present, and immediately turned the gathering on to a business footing, as against the 'hail fellow, well met' atmosphere that had prevailed before.

It did not take long for her to get totally immersed in the meeting's cause, and she forgot her role of helper, as she became deeply interested in the different points of view being discussed, and she learnt more about the island's way of life in those two hours than she had done since her arrival six months ago.

It appeared that Peter was not the only one whose livelihood was threatened. There was an odd-looking man who spoke in what Edwina would have called University English, but who wore an old faded shirt over equally faded jeans, and whose age Edwina found difficult to pinpoint, but who certainly was a senior citizen, who sold crabs and anything else the fishermen bestowed upon him after a particularly successful trip, and Edwina gathered, as this was his only source of income, that he had not unnaturally sided with the conservationists, only his conservation was a little more on the personal side than on the actual definition of the word. The man was addressed as 'Fishy' and as Edwina was not provided with any other name, his remarks were credited to that name with a small question mark by the diligent Edwina when recording.

The 'easy chair' brigade consisted of Colonel Melway, whom Edwina would have recognised even if Peter had not made a quick introduction at the start of the meeting, a tall, stout man, with the inevitable military bearing, and whose staccato way of talking soon singled him out as a presence to be reckoned with, his, 'I'll have no nonsense,' tone of voice would soon put any doubts on this score to flight. He towered over Martin Canfourth, the man Peter had said was hoping to get the marina, and who was a small bespectacled rather timid-looking man, with an apologetic way of speaking, and Edwina could not help comparing him against Damon Morven's harsh dictatorial utterings, and felt a twinge of depression at the comparison, if it could be called that.

Lastly, there was Peter, who had as much to lose as anyone else there, from the man who hawked crabs for a living to the old couple, a Mr and Mrs Scalway, who beachcombed for conch shells and any other shells to make into items of jewellery to sell to the tourists in the more lucrative southern end of the island. The point that they also depended on free access to the beach for their living was not made, but judging by the anxiousness displayed on their weatherbeaten features such a fact was unnecessary.

It soon became apparent to Edwina that most of the company present were against the idea of big business moving into their small community, and who could blame them?

A Mrs Foley, a small sparse woman, dressed in Bohemian style with rows of beads that swung in fascinating swirls as she grabbed the floor and started expounding on the beauties of their unspoilt part of the island, was given a sharp set-down by the

Colonel before she could get into her stride, much
to everyone else's approval, for it was unfortunately obvious that she was the kind of woman
who was anti anything, and Edwina, who was
having difficulty at that stage of the proceedings in
what to record and what to leave out, had to make
a hasty ruling through the Colonel's muttered
expletive of 'Stupid woman!' as Mrs Foley was
shouted down and forced to resume her seat
again.

The discussion got quite heated now and again,
but Martin Canfourth's quiet but firm intervention
soon brought things under control again, as he
explained his reasons for wanting to keep the Star
Point project on modest lines, and how the marina
he had in mind ought to enhance the island scenery
and not abuse it, which gained everyone's approval. If a marina was going to be built, and
according to the consent given, it was, then they
would far rather Martin Canfourth's plans were put
into action, since it went without saying that he
intended to watch over the interests of the local
population.

There was only, Martin Canfourth concluded,
the salient point of getting his plans accepted. He
had the backing of several business friends of his,
financially, that was, so there should be no problem
there. The outcome rested entirely with the powers
that be.

There were more rumblings on this last statement, and Mrs Foley took advantage of the lapse of
the speakers to expound once more on her theme.

'Speaking as an artist—' was as far as she got, before she had to turn and glare at a man next to her who stated, 'If she's an artist, I'm a jet pilot!' another irreverent remark that Edwina had to hastily remove from the records.

A Mr Jocelyn then started to outline the kind of tourist the other type of marina would attract, which was hardly necessary, seeing that this was the main reason for the meeting, but he intended to have his way. He had, he said prosaically, nothing against a boating complex, for yachtsmen only, but would fight tooth and nail against an entertainment complex. There was plenty of that type of amusement in the south, thank you, and more on this theme.

The Colonel then took the floor. 'I think everyone is jumping to conclusions,' he said, barking out his words, and pausing to glare around him as if daring anyone to contradict him. 'How do we know just what Morven's got in mind?'

Edwina, busily recording, thought that Peter's assumption that it was Damon Morven they were up against had been correct, and this gave her an added reason for her presence; anything she could do to upset that man's haughty aplomb would be well worth the trouble.

'He's not actually said he was turning the area into an entertainment zone,' continued the Colonel. 'The thing is to get together and compare notes and see just what he has in mind.'

'Once he gets that land, the marina will be conveniently forgotten,' said a surly-looking man in a bright red shirt and tan shorts. 'Money talks,' he added sneeringly.

'He'll have to comply with the regulations,' the Colonel barked back. 'No matter what he pays for it, and that goes for anyone else,' he added darkly.

'An open meeting with all the interested bodies, you mean?' Peter asked.

The Colonel nodded. 'Well, just the two now. The Astra group have pulled out, and that leaves this group and Morven Enterprises,' he said.

This caused a round of mutterings from the assembly on the lines of 'know when they're beaten, fat chance we've got,' and more on the same theme, then Mr Joycelyn asked the sixty-four-thousand-dollar question. 'Whose side are you on, Colonel?'

'No one's side,' Colonel Melway retorted smartly, his stiff features echoing his outrage at having his motives questioned. 'By the end of next week, I shall tell you. I want to know a lot more about what Morven intends to do with the extra land he's asked for, before I give my blessing to the scheme.'

'What extra land?' demanded the man called Fishy, and he was followed by the same outcry from the others.

'Not Ludlow's Cave!' Mrs Foley shrieked. 'Oh, no, Colonel, he can't have that! It's just below my cottage!' she wailed.

Colonel Melway flung her an exasperated look. 'If it's just a marina he's building, then you've nothing to worry about,' he said brusquely, and turned to Peter. 'As far as I know it's south of Star Point, but I don't know how far up he's coming,' he said. 'But I'll fight for your access rights no matter who I give my support to,' he assured Peter.

Peter nodded glumly at this kindliness, but he did not look too assured of success in this particular venture.

The meeting ended shortly after this, with the members drifting off home, but the Colonel adjourned to the bar with Peter and Martin, and a reluctant Edwina was persuaded to make a fourth, with the Colonel's insistence on buying her some refreshment in thanks for the help she had given.

The talk naturally centred on the subject that they had just been discussing, with the Colonel reiterating his support for Peter should Morven Enterprises win the day.

When the Colonel went to replenish their glasses, shrugging away Peter's offer of drinks on the house, Martin said to Peter, 'We couldn't hope to match Morven's offer if he's determined to have that contract. Whatever we offer, he'll top it, and we can't play that sort of game. Still, if it's just a question of suitability, then we stand as good a chance as anyone,' he added brightly. 'Seems to me, Peter, we don't stand a hope if we lose the Colonel's support. Just how friendly is he with Morven? do you know?' he asked.

Peter shrugged. 'Only that they move in the same big business circles. But you're right, the Colonel will have the last say in the matter. He's got the right contacts in the right places, and this is his territory,' he added in a low voice, as the Colonel joined them with the refills.

With the topic of the marina exhausted, for the time being anyway, the talk roamed on other subjects, and the Colonel set himself out to entertain Edwina, while Peter and Martin got immersed in their favourite subject, game fishing.

The Colonel was interested in Edwina. He knew that she was a newcomer to the Islands, and was curious as to why such a presentable young lady should have chosen to work in what could be described as the backwoods, well away from the city lights.

Edwina smilingly replied that it wasn't quite as odd as it seemed. She was no stranger to that part of the world, although it was some time ago. She had, she told the Colonel, spent the first seven years of her life in Nassau.

'Nassau, eh?' Colonel Melway exclaimed with raised brows. 'You wouldn't by any chance have attended Miss Pinkerton's Academy, would you?' he asked with twinkling eyes.

Edwina grinned as the memory of that prim young ladies' school's owner came to mind, and confirmed his query.

'Aha!' Colonel Melway retorted in triumph. 'You were one of the Embassy children!'

Edwina knew what the next question would be, and was not too sure that she wanted that part of it brought out, since it would involve the fact that she had a sister, and that might conceivably lead to other things that were better not aired at this point of time, but she was saved by the Colonel suddenly spotting a newcomer to the bar and waving his arm in that direction and calling, 'Over here, Morven!'

Edwina's relaxed stance stiffened as her dismayed eyes followed the direction of the Colonel's arm, held up to attract the attention of the man he was hailing, and she wondered if she could possibly slip away before he joined them, but it would have been too obvious, as she was sure he had seen her.

'I thought it might be a good idea if we had a word with Morven,' Colonel Melway said to Peter and Martin, 'but I wasn't sure he could make it this evening,' he added, as Damon Morven reached their table, his hard grey eyes resting momentarily on Edwina, then he nodded abruptly at the Colonel.

'You know Knight and Canfourth,' the Colonel said, 'and this is Miss Rosewall, Knight's secretary, who is helping us out in the office line.'

Again Edwina experienced the cold gaze of Damon Morven, and held herself in readiness for what she was sure was going to be an exposure as to the type of woman the group had unwittingly drawn into their centre, but to her astonishment there was no such denouncement, and in a daze she heard him acknowledge the introduction with a dry impersonal, 'Miss Rosewall,' and offered his hand for her to shake, and, slightly stunned, Edwina was forced to follow convention and take the proffered hand as the Colonel completed the introduction.

Not a muscle on that strong hard face of his had moved as he gravely shook hands with Edwina, but his strength of grip told her that he had not forgotten her, and Edwina was only too relieved when the grip was released and she was able to move back from him and resume her seat at the table, well away from the chair that had been placed next to the Colonel's seat for him to take.

While the men got down to business, Edwina tried to make some sense of Damon Morven's strange behaviour. Being the type of man he was, he was not likely to let any opportunity pass in exposing a woman he thought of as a gold-digger, and he was not likely to be plagued by any other considerations, such as finer feelings. As far as she was concerned, he didn't have any! A thought then crossed her mind that almost made her grin in appreciation of its subtleness. This was the opposition when all was said and done, and he probably thought she was planning to abscond with the subscription fund in the not too distant future, and would be wishing her success in the venture.

He would, no doubt, she thought shrewdly, drop a few well-intentioned hints to Colonel Melway to steer clear of her. He could not afford to upset the Colonel! Neither could Peter, she thought worriedly, as her eyes rested on the men around the table, still talking, or at least the Colonel was doing most of the talking and the rest listening, including Edwina's arch-enemy, whose cold eyes at that precise moment wandered in her direction, and she wondered how often this had occurred, for she had been lost in her own thoughts since the discussion began.

The thought was not a comfortable one, and as soon as there was a pause in the conversation, Edwina got up swiftly. 'If you gentlemen will excuse me,' she murmured, and took her leave before the Colonel could object to her leaving the company, or at least making sure that she would be returning.

As it was just before closing time, the latter hope was extremely unlikely, for the meeting would soon have to end, unless Peter took them through to his private quarters, but Edwina thought this was an improbability. The atmosphere had not been an exactly congenial one, in spite of the Colonel's efforts, for Peter had too much to lose, and that went for most of the members of the conservationist group.

Once in Peter's quarters, Edwina headed for her bedroom and got ready for her shower before going to bed. If Damon Morven intended to be present at the meeting the Colonel had promised to arrange the following week, then she would have to come up with some excuse for her non-attendance. She did not trust that man one inch. If things went against him, she was sure he could turn quite nasty, and she didn't need a horoscope to tell her who would be on the receiving end of his frustrated hopes!

The following morning, Peter was exceptionally quiet at breakfast, and Edwina had practically to prise conversation out of him. 'Why on earth did Colonel Melway ask that man to drop in last night?' she asked Peter eventually, when no information was offered.

Peter pulled a wry face. 'I think he'd got some bee in his bonnet that we might get together on some sort of communal programme,' he said with a heavy sigh. 'However, that's out. I gathered he only turned up to please the Colonel. He needs his support as much as we do, but there'll be no sharing of ideas as far as he's concerned. It looks as if our fears of him turning the place into a glorified tourist attraction are justified,' he added gloomily.

There was silence while he refilled his coffee cup. 'The Colonel asked him straight out what he intended to do with that extra land he's asked for,' he continued, 'and whatever it is, he's keeping it close to his chest,' he added darkly. 'Said that if his plans were accepted there'd be a blueprint up on the town hall's board.' He frowned into his coffee cup. 'I had the distinct feeling that he would have told the Colonel if they'd been alone, and that means that whatever he's got in mind, it won't suit the conservationists,' he ended meaningly.

On that gloomy note, he left Edwina and went on his morning rounds, and Edwina wished that there was something that she could do to help, but Julia had effectively quashed any hope in that direction. It would have been better for Peter, Edwina thought, if she had taken the next plane home, since she was sure that Damon Morven was going to use her, through Julia's indiscretion, to get at the Colonel, and it could very well work. The Colonel belonged to the old school, and had values long forgotten in that day and age. One little word in his ear would be enough to swing his support Morven's way. The Colonel did not know that Edwina was related to Peter, but one hint that she was sharing Peter's private quarters would be enough, she thought worriedly, to turn the scales.

Just after ten, Peter looked in on Edwina, now using the office section to type up her notes on the previous evening's meeting, and feeling a depressed certainty that it was all to no avail, and she might as well not bother, but she needed something to do.

'I'm off with Martin,' Peter told her. 'Be back around fourish. We might as well make as much use of our amenities while we can,' he added sombrely, echoing Edwina's thoughts on the matter, and leaving her even more depressed.

By ten-thirty she had finished, and went through to her room to collect a cardigan. She needed to be out in the cool fresh air, for the hotel was situated on an incline that overlooked the bay, and received the benefit of whatever sea breezes were going, even on an extremely hot day.

Edwina had just got to the steps that led down to the beach when she heard her name called, and turned back to find Damon Morven coming towards her.

Her first instinct was to keep going, and at a much faster rate, but she managed to quell this natural but rather cowardly action, and stood her ground until he joined her.

'I'm afraid Mr Knight's out on a fishing trip,' she said coldly. 'I'll take a message if you want to leave one,' she added reluctantly, for she was supposed to be Peter's secretary, she told herself.

'It's not Knight I want to see,' Damon Morven said, walking on past her and indicating with an autocratic sweep of his arm that she should walk with him, and together they descended the few steps to the beach.

'So,' Damon said to her, when they reached the firm shingle of the beach. 'You've joined the opposition, have you?'

Edwina brushed away a strand of hair that had clung to her cheek, and gave him the sort of look she would have given a man who was making a nuisance of himself, and whose attentions she was definitely not going to encourage. 'I work for Mr Knight,' she said coldly. 'I lost my job, if you remember,' she reminded him icily.

'That you would have got back if you'd asked for it,' he replied in a smooth too assured voice that she took immediate exception to.

'Oh, was that what you were offering me?' she said in a voice that scarcely bothered to hide her scepticism. 'Oh, well, never mind, it was all for the best, wasn't it? I'm enjoying my work here.'

'Don't push your luck,' Damon growled warningly. 'I could have burst your pretty balloon last night, but I chose not to.'

Edwina's eyes flashed. Now they were coming to it!

'I said nothing because I felt you might be useful to me,' he continued blandly. 'Like keeping me informed on the opposition's moves. Unfortunately it's not a question of money. If it was, I'd win hands down, but I want that contract, Miss Rosewall, and you won't find me ungenerous either.'

Edwina stood staring at him. He presented a very handsome figure of a man—tall, lean, his dark brown hair brushed back from a high intellectual forehead, with slivers of grey showing at the sides. He would be around the thirty-five mark, she thought absently, as her gaze swept over his immaculate tan lightweight suit, with cream shirt and matching tan tie.

That she was taking her time in assessing him gave him some amusement, and she had a feeling that given time he would have asked her if he passed muster, but she was not going to give him that pleasure. A saying then went through her mind, something on the lines of 'publish and be damned', and she wished she could say just that, but there was Peter to consider. There might still be a chance that he retained access to the beach even if this man did get the contract, and she could not risk giving vent to her feelings. 'I owe an allegiance to Mr Knight, Mr Morven,' she said, 'and it doesn't pay to change horses in midstream,' she added on a sweet note.

'Two can play at that game, Miss Rosewall,' he replied harshly, all amusement gone. 'Okay, so I annoyed you, and Knight soothed your ruffled feathers, but you've chosen the wrong horse, you know. Knight isn't going to have much of a business when I take over. I'll get rough if I have to. I'm offering you a job. You either take it or be a fool and turn it down. If you do turn it down, then by the time I'm finished with you, you won't be able to get a job in the whole of the Caribbean. I'll personally see to that!'

Edwina somehow held on to her temper, but two bright spots on her cheeks betrayed her feelings. 'As I've said,' she got out between clenched teeth, 'I already have a job—'

That was as far as he allowed her to get before he cut in roughly, 'As Knight's secretary—yes, so you said. He's never had a secretary before, has he? I know a little bit more about this part of the Island than you imagine, so don't try that cloak of respectability on me, I'm wise to it.'

His hard grey eyes bored into hers, and then his hand caught hers in a hurtful grip that intensified as she tried to snatch it away. Then he slowly turned her hand over to expose the soft palm and gently ran his lean fingers over the firm soft area, making Edwina's heartbeats increase rapidly. There had been an intimacy there that had shocked her. 'But then you're special, aren't you?' he said softly. 'Even a confirmed bachelor like Knight lost his head over you, didn't he? You're living in his private quarters, aren't you?' he added silkily.

Edwina was still fighting off the chaotic emotions his still stroking fingers had aroused in her, but she gasped at the implied innuendo and raised her free hand to deliver a sharp slap at that arrogant face so close to hers, but she was denied even this consolation, for he caught it in mid-swing, and she was then completely imprisoned by him.

She was too furiously angry to plead with him to release her, and her lovely eyes blazed back at him, the tawny gold specks brilliant in their hatred of this man who had dared to assault her, not only physically, but orally as well.

'Magnificent!' Damon Morven murmured in sheer appreciation. 'I feel like a big game hunter confronted by my first tigress. Shall I shoot you, I wonder, or shall I carry you off home and tame you?'

He suddenly released her, and Edwina stood rubbing her wrists where his hands had bruised her flesh and glowered at him.

'Oh, yes, as I thought. You're worthy of my mettle,' he said softly, then shrugged. 'Unfortunately, you're stupid, just like all women. Knight is looking out for you now, but you haven't the sense to see that he won't be able to provide for you for much longer. I gave you your chance. You can forget what I said about a job. I've changed my mind,' and with that caustic comment he abruptly left her.

CHAPTER FIVE

By the time Peter got back, Edwina had regained her composure. She had decided that there was little point in telling Peter of her confrontation with Damon Morven. There was nothing that he could do about it, anyway. It was now a case of waiting to see which way the cat jumped, or in this case the big game hunter!

The Colonel would be the next on his list, Edwina was certain that would be his next move, and she felt depressed over that, because she liked the Colonel, but she knew she would have to steel herself for a snub should they meet again. Not that she could imagine him dealing out such treatment, he was too much of a gentleman for that, but he would probably be most embarrassed, and that somehow made it worse from Edwina's point of view.

She ought to at least warn Peter of that eventuality, she thought worriedly, but she couldn't. Not without telling him what had transpired between her and Damon Morven, and embarrassment wouldn't be the word should Peter find out what that man had hinted at!

There was but one solution open to her, and that was to accept Stanley's offer to accompany Julia to New York. Edwina would hate it. She knew only too well what Julia's idea of entertainment was, but beggars couldn't be choosers, she told herself stoically, and it would solve a lot of problems. Perhaps she could get a job in the States? From what Damon Morven had said, she was not likely to have much luck in obtaining any sort of work where she was, and he was not the type of man to make idle threats.

Tomorrow, she told herself, she would go and see Julia and Stanley, and accept the offer.

'Go with Julia to the States?' Peter said incredulously, after Edwina informed him of her decision at dinner that evening. 'You'll hate it, you know you will!' he said. 'Stanley's going to be busy, remember, and you'll have to put up with madam's whims, and whatever else she might get up to,' he added darkly.

Edwina sighed. Those were exactly her sentiments, but needs must. 'Oh, I'm not worried that she'll step out of line again,' she said quickly. 'She had quite a fright, you know, and she really is fond of Stanley. She's not likely to risk doing anything silly again.'

Peter gave a snort of derision at this, he plainly did not think it was possible. 'Well, think about it,' he advised her, then said indignantly, 'I thought you were really interested in our fight.'

Edwina sighed inwardly. She was, too interested, and too involved, in fact a whopping big liability that Peter could well do without—but of course he didn't know that, she thought sadly, as her glance rested momentarily on the long-sleeved blouse that she had had to wear because of the bruise marks that were still very much in evidence on her wrists. Damon Morven's calling card!

There was no answer to Peter's query, of course, not one good enough, she knew, so she said nothing, but just played with her sweet, for which she had lost all appetite.

Something about the droop of her slim shoulders reached through to Peter and he patted her on the shoulder. 'Well, you do what you want to do. Either way, it won't make much difference. Come to think of it,' he said musingly, 'it might be a good idea at that. I didn't like the way Morven was eyeing you last night, and I don't want you to get mixed up with him, not after dear Julia's introduction to the family where he was concerned. He'll think you're fair game, and I'm not having that.'

Edwina knew exactly what Damon Morven thought of her, and she didn't need Peter to tell her, or warn her, come to that, but she was glad she had not upset him by her decision to leave.

It was nice to know that in spite of how much Peter had to lose he would put her first, and this thought went a little way to console her for what she was sure was going to be a miserable time ahead of her.

To Peter's surprise, Colonel Melway dropped in on them that evening asking for Edwina's secretarial help at a meeting he was due to attend the following morning, if Peter could spare her, that was, and a bemused Edwina heard Peter say that he had no objection, if Edwina hadn't.

It did mean that she would have to put off her visit to Stanley and Julia until the afternoon, and as she was not exactly looking forward to the visit, she had no objection to putting it off, even if it was only for a few hours.

'I hope you don't mind, my dear,' the Colonel said, the following morning when he called for her, 'but I was suddenly reminded of this meeting—got a shocking memory these days, I'm afraid. Used to have a secretary, you know, but when Caters retired I didn't replace her. Don't do all that much to warrant one now, but seeing you yesterday reminded me of how it used to be. For instance, this meeting, she'd have got it all taped for me, papers ready and all that sort of thing, you know, and I could cheerfully forget about the whole thing afterwards, because she would have typed the minutes for me.' He settled Edwina in his car, and got in himself and turned on the ignition. 'So, as I said,' he went on, as he steered the big car out of the drive of the Haven, 'seeing you yesterday brought it all back to me, and as this is a meeting that I ought to have a record of, I wondered if you'd be good enough to oblige me.' He gave Edwina a quick stare from under his bushy eyebrows, 'I don't suppose Knight has all that much work for you, either, has he?' he added brightly.

Edwina was forced to concede this point, but wondered if Damon Morven had said anything to him, yet if he had, she couldn't see the Colonel seeking her help for this or any other work!

As the car continued down the potholed roads,

drifting along on its well sprung interior, Edwina had a sudden idea that she was being given a golden opportunity to spike Damon Morven's guns. 'Well, I don't really work for Peter,' she explained. 'We're related, you know, he's by way of being a distant cousin of mine, so I'm just filling in time at the Haven until something turns up.' She thought it best not to mention that she had worked at the Splendour.

'Well, bless my soul,' exclaimed the Colonel. 'Well, that explains it! I couldn't see why you should want to stay at the Haven, not even in a working capacity. It's out of the run of an ordinary hotel, fishermen and all that sort of thing, I mean,' he added jovially.

They were now approaching the small township that divided the north of the island from the south, and Colonel Melway pulled up in front of a big white structure that had been a cinema, and was now doing duty as the town hall.

After assisting Edwina out of the car in a fashion that made her feel like a pensioner, he delved into the back seats of the car and produced a briefcase. 'Got some data in here,' he said, 'that we'll sort out while we're waiting—someone's always late,' he added dryly, as he shepherded Edwina into the close atmosphere of the building, stuffy in the heat, in spite of the fans swirling overhead.

To Edwina's relief, the meeting was not a public one, for she was led to a small office at the end of a long clinically white passageway, where they found three men already gathered.

The Colonel made a short, 'Miss Rosewall—er—acting secretary,' introduction, before they got down to the meeting, that appeared to Edwina to be some sort of a financial transaction, and she was instructed by the Colonel to just take down names of the companies which would be read out to her, and the comments passed.

There had been no time to study the papers in the Colonel's briefcase, but he provided her with a list of companies that they would be dealing with, so there was no problem for Edwina, all she had to do was to record such phrases as 'Sell' or 'hang on' and in some cases 'buy'.

It was not long before she realised that the Colonel was some kind of a financial wizard, and was there more to give advice than to receive it. She also noticed that there were several Morven Enterprises listed on the sheet in front of her, and it was always 'buy' when these were referred to. As Peter had said, Damon Morven was a very big fish indeed!

The meeting ended shortly after noon, and the grateful Colonel offered to take Edwina to lunch at a small but good restaurant he knew on the way to the Haven. She accepted, knowing that this was his way of saying 'thank you'.

'It's the least I can do,' the Colonel said happily, as he ushered her back into the car. 'It was just like old times, and I know I should have a secretary for these meetings, my memory being what it is, but I didn't fancy hiring a stranger from an agency. Besides,' he added with a twinkle in his eye, 'we don't want to start a slide on the market, do we? Could cause havoc if the wrong person got hold of some of that information—have to watch points, you know.'

Edwina felt flattered that he trusted her, and that he did not regard her as a stranger, yet she had only met him the day before.

The 'small' restaurant that the Colonel told Edwina that he would be taking her to was not so small, not from outward appearances anyway, and was a building that Edwina had often passed on her way back to the Haven on her off duty periods at the Splendour. She had always thought that it was a private residence, and as the Colonel escorted her through the ornate glass doors to the restaurant and her feet sunk into the plush carpeting, she wondered what kind of prices were charged, and suspected it was a high price that the Colonel was paying for her services.

The murmur of voices reached them as they went through yet another set of glass doors, and then they were in the restaurant, the tables laid with snowy white table cloths on which silver cutlery gleamed, and each table was adorned with a small bouquet of fresh flowers in a silver vase at its centre.

The room was not overcrowded, indeed the placing of the tables were so arranged that maximum space was allotted to each table, heightening Edwina's suspicions of the high tariff this exclusive place would charge.

There were four empty tables in the room, and a

waiter materialising out of nowhere gave the Colonel a reverent-sounding welcome, and waited for him to choose his table, and after a brief glance round the Colonel chose one close to the windows the other side of the room.

It was not until they had passed the first two tables that were occupied, and came to a third that was set slightly back in an alcove, that Edwina found herself looking at the back of Damon Morven, seated opposite another man, and her steps faltered slightly as she followed the Colonel's lead to the chosen table, and whether it was the approach of two people that had made Damon turn his head in time to see Edwina's startled reaction at coming across him like that, or whether it was some sort of sixth sense he possessed where she was concerned, Edwina didn't know, but she was thankful that the Colonel had chosen that particular table well away from the alcove.

The Colonel spotted Damon while he was seating Edwina at the table and raised his hand in salutation, then settled at the table. He was not to know that Edwina would have preferred to sit with her back to the rest of the room, and that included Damon Morven, of course, but as it was, she was facing the wretched man. However, she managed to edge her chair a little to the left so that the Colonel's ample figure partially blocked her from the rest of the room. She could only hope that Morven left before them, and there was no possibility of him joining them.

After consulting the gilt-edged menu, that held a

vast array of dishes, Edwina settled for an avocado pear for starters, followed by Boeuf Stroganoff, a dish that the Colonel assured her he could well recommend, then she settled back, but with little hope of enjoying the meal, not in the near proximity of the man who seemed to dodge her footsteps like an evil genie, but she was able to make a reasonable showing in consideration of the Colonel's feelings.

They were halfway through their lunch when to Edwina's dismay she saw Damon making for their table, and picked up her glass to take a hasty sip of her wine to avoid having to look straight at him as he approached the table.

For one awful moment she wondered whether he had chosen this moment to denounce her to the Colonel, but as she replaced the glass on to the table she heard him say casually, 'We don't often see you here these days, Colonel.'

'Not often I get the chance of entertaining a charming young lady to lunch,' Colonel Melway replied jovially. 'I note that the standard is still up to scratch,' he added appreciatively, as he urged Edwina to get on with her meal.

'I trust you are also enjoying your lunch, Miss Rosewall?' Damon asked in a smooth voice.

Edwina wished she could tell him she would have done but for his presence, but she said, 'Very much, thank you,' in a very polite voice, the kind of voice that one used when thanking a disliked relation for a perfectly awful weekend.

She knew that he was aware of the underlying

nuances in her tone by the way his eyes narrowed, and she did not miss the way his glance went instinctively to her wrists, no doubt hoping to see the mark of the bruises from their last meeting, or perhaps he was giving her a warning of more to come, she thought uneasily, as she heard him say, 'Well, see you,' a remark that somehow embraced Edwina as much as the Colonel, but with veiled undertones where she was concerned.

There was a brief silence after he had gone, during which time their sweet, an ice cream gateau, was served, but Edwina hardly registered the fact that the waiter was there, her eyes were on the tall straight back of Damon Morven as he left the restaurant.

'He's not such a bad fellow, you know,' the Colonel said to Edwina, unwittingly letting her know that he had noticed her absorption, not to mention her dislike of the man. 'A bit unbending, but then he's a business man. Knows what he wants, but he's as straight as they come. But you're right to be wary of him. He's not much time for women—er, not in the business line, that is,' he added, as he hastily applied himself to his sweet.

'So I've found out,' Edwina said dryly, as she picked up her dessert spoon and took a spoonful of what looked like a delicious concoction.

The Colonel swallowed another spoonful and stared at her. 'Had a brush with him, have you?' he asked abruptly, 'I rather thought there was something in the wind,' and at Edwina's sudden tightening of the lips, he added hastily, 'Not my business, my dear, but if there's anything I can do—' and left it at that. He was obviously curious, but too much of a gentleman to probe further.

Edwina looked at him. In many ways he reminded her of her father. He had that same air of assumed naïveté—assumed, that was, until action was called for. He was nobody's fool, and his manner of putting on a little-boy-lost look did not fool Edwina for one minute, as her father's hadn't but it had fooled Julia on more than one occasion and it had taken her a long time to get the hang of it, much to her cost.

Even the way he had tucked into his sweet, for he obviously had a sweet tooth, there again like her father, who attacked such delicacies much like a ten-year-old boy, made her swallow hastily, suddenly realising how much she missed his strong guidance and commonsense way of looking at situations.

'Well, not me exactly—my sister, in fact,' she said, having finally decided to reveal all. She trusted the Colonel, and this was probably the last chance she would get to tell her side of the story.

'Bless my soul! You've a sister here?' he exclaimed.

Edwina nodded, and once again she couldn't understand why the name of Rosewall hadn't awakened memories of Julia's wedding. It might never have happened, according to Damon Morven and the Colonel. 'She's married now,' she said, giving the Colonel a slightly perplexed look. 'It was about six months ago. It took place back home, but it was reported in the local papers,' she said, gently prodding his memory.

The Colonel still looked blank. 'Don't read local gossip, my dear,' he explained. 'Who did she marry?'

Edwina gave Stanley's name, and where they were living now.

'Oh, the oil chappie!' exclaimed the Colonel. 'I'm with you now. Heard he'd married someone from the U.K. So it was your sister, was it?'

It was not all he was going to hear, Edwina thought darkly, if Damon Morven had his way. 'Julia came out here with me,' she explained, 'and of course this is where she met Stanley.' She hesitated. This was going to be the tricky part of it all, she thought miserably, and swallowed. 'Well, before she met Stanley, she worked at one of Damon Morven's hotels.' She paused, then went on quickly, because she sensed that the Colonel was about to remonstrate that he had no wish to discomfit her. 'She—well—she made a fool of herself,' she said quietly.

The Colonel nodded understandingly. 'Over Morven, you mean?' he said, but it was more of a statement than a question, proving that Edwina's summing up of him had been right on target. 'Well, my dear, that's not so unusual, you know. There's plenty that's flung their cap at that windmill.'

Edwina nodded. 'I rather gathered that,' she said in what she hoped sounded like a dry comment, but she was beginning to get embarrassed. It was kind of the Colonel to make it all sound so matter-of-fact, when it wasn't. 'I'm afraid she received no encouragement, so I can't blame Mr Morven for adopting the attitude he has towards me. You see, I was stupid enough to go and apologise for her behaviour. I knew an apology was called for, but—' her voice tailed off.

'Say no more, my dear,' said the Colonel, patting her hand. 'I'm not such an old buffer that I have to have the t's crossed. Thinks you're on the same bent, does he?' he asked kindly.

Edwina stared at him. He had got it in a nutshell! 'Why, that's exactly what he does think!' she exclaimed.

'Well, don't worry, my dear. I'll soon scotch any rumours of that kind if I get to hear of any,' he assured her bluffly.

Edwina's gratitude shone in her lovely eyes, and she fervently wished there was something else she could do for the Colonel. She felt as if a load had been taken off her shoulders, and wished she did not have to go to New York with Julia, but for Peter's sake it was better if she was off the scene. He would stand a better chance of getting that access he wanted if she wasn't around. Damon Morven would think the Colonel was just an old sentimental fool who had been taken in by a schemer, and her continuous presence at the Haven, under what he thought of as the innocuous title of secretary, would only serve to strengthen his suspicions.

'Now, tell me what branch of the Service your father worked in,' the Colonel said brightly, obviously thinking it was time to change the subject, as their coffee was served.

Edwina told him about Sir Charles, and before she could expound further on the theme, the Colonel exclaimed, 'Chubby Charlie? Good gracious! Did time together at Winchester—at least I did time, I was his fag!' he added, with a comical grimace. 'Pompous as they come, and didn't change any, either. Wasn't a bit surprised to hear he went into the Diplomatic. Ran into him, of course, on several occasions, but never did have much time for him. He was still inclined to treat me as his underling. So your father went back with him when he retired, did he?' in a manner that showed that he was plainly mystified as to why anyone should choose to stay in such a person's employment.

Edwina smiled as she caught the surprise in his voice. 'Yes, well, Sir Charles had decided to write his memoirs, and I think Father and Mother thought it was time they settled down, so they jumped at the idea of going home.'

'Write his memoirs!' the Colonel spluttered, highly indignant. 'What's he got to write about? The only thing worthy of note in his career was when they got the Embassy dinners mixed up and served a Chinese dinner to the American Ambassador!'

Edwina could have clapped her hands in sheer enjoyment. How often had her father related that same story!

'Well, I'm blessed!' exclaimed the Colonel,

absentmindedly refilling his coffee cup and forgetting to refill Edwina's. Then he blinked. 'Oh, I do beg your pardon,' he said hastily, and quickly made up for his omission. 'Now if he'd seen a bit of service I could understand it. The nearest he got to the front was to sign chits for extra warm clothing for the Desert Rats. The nights were pretty chilly, you know, I know because I was one of them,' he added musingly.

Edwina was about to seek more enlightenment on this theme, when the Colonel's fist thumped the table, making her jump and scattering the remaining cutlery. 'No! Dammit, I won't have it!' he exclaimed. 'I'll do it!'

Edwina blinked. Do what? she wondered.

The Colonel came out of his reverie and gave her a wry grin. 'Sorry my dear—got carried away. Better explain,' he said gruffly. 'Was approached a few years ago by the Principal of the school. Asked me if I'd care to write my memoirs. You know, the usual thing, of interest to the school and all that twaddle. Was too busy then to oblige,' he frowned, 'Not too busy now, eh?' he barked at Edwina. 'Kept the records, always meaning to get down to it one day,' he added musingly, and glanced at her. 'Couldn't hope to beat him to it, of course, should be published now. He's had enough of a start on it.'

Edwina smiled. 'Well, he doesn't appear to be in any hurry,' she said lightly. 'He treats it as a kind of hobby, much to my father's dismay. He's still wading through reams of matter, so you haven't any worry there, not for a few years anyway.'

The Colonel gave a delighted chuckle. 'We'll beat him to it, then,' he said enthusiastically.

Edwina was not too sure what he meant by 'we', but she thought he was referring to a few of his colleagues. However, she was not long left in doubt.

The Colonel gave her a look of interrogation. 'Well?' he demanded. 'Are you with me?'

Edwina blinked. Did he mean—?

'Look!' the Colonel said gruffly. 'I'll need a secretary, won't I? I'm offering you the job. Can't think of anyone else I'd rather have to help me with the work,' he added hopefully.

'I—well, I'd love to.' It was out before Edwina could retract the words, and at the Colonel's delighted smile at her acceptance, she knew she could not go back on her words. She didn't want to, she wanted to help him with the book, but she still wasn't sure about Peter—not that he would stop her, he'd be as delighted as she was about the job, but there were a few things he didn't know. Then a thought came to her that made things right for her. Peter needed the Colonel's support and she would be in a perfect position to route for his cause, wouldn't she? It wasn't sneaky. She was on the side of the conservationists, and the Colonel knew that, so it wasn't as if she was going to carry on some undercover action.

Edwina's step was light as the Colonel escorted her out of the restaurant. She didn't have to accompany Julia to New York. She had a job, but far better than that, she had a champion in the

Colonel, and she knew she could rely on him for her future security. Eat your heart out, Damon Morven! she thought happily, as the Colonel drove her back to the Haven.

CHAPTER SIX

EDWINA walked down the steps from the Haven to the beach, to a place she had chosen for her sunbathing. It was just under the overhang of the hotel and not too sheltered from the sun to prevent her from receiving the warm rays.

It was exactly a week after she had begun to work for the Colonel, and the job was all she had hoped it would be. She had often thought of her father as she had sorted out the Colonel's reminiscences, faithfully recorded in days gone by, more for his own amusement than for public perusal, but here was a story worth the telling, and she knew her father would give an enviable sigh did he but know what she was doing. It was perhaps as well that he didn't, she had thought with a smile, as she recalled his sheer frustration at the task in front of him, and the non-co-operation of Sir Charles, for he had often remarked to Edwina that if he didn't get down to it, it would turn out to be his obituary rather than a biographical study!

A movement in the far distance caught her eye, and she waved as she recognised the thin wiry figure of Fishy setting up his stall, such as it was, that consisted of a single plank upheld by two large boulders that were part of the natural terrain. Simplicity was his motto, she thought smilingly, as she settled back on her lilo. Now there, she was sure, was another story to be told. Fishy intrigued her. She had once asked Peter what his real name was, but he had not known, just said that he had always been called that, ever since he had first appeared out of the blue several years ago.

The warm rays of the sun sank into her recumbent form and she closed her eyes in sheer pleasure. Fishy was no ordinary man. He was exceedingly well educated, and Edwina wondered if he had been a teacher, perhaps even a don who had decided to opt out of scholastic pursuits to spend the rest of his life in the sunlit Caribbean. He probably lived in one of the old shacks she had seen dotted about the coastline. He wouldn't need much, he had enough food to live on, and what he made from the crabs and fish he was given would probably go on keeping that old pipe of his well stoked up. She only hoped he would be able to go on living in this fashion.

She frowned. She didn't want to think of things like that. She had spent all that week in industrious work, and now she could relax. She had earned it. Her thoughts then turned to Julia, now safely in New York, and having, as Edwina had known she would, a very hectic time, pausing once or twice in that first week to ring Edwina and keep her informed of her doings. It had amused Edwina, for when she had lived only a mile or so away from her, Julia had never made any attempt to draw her into her new-found social circle—not that Edwina would have allowed this to happen, but as soon as she was at a distance from Edwina, she seemed to feel the need to keep in communication with her. For all Julia's professed scepticism of family ties, her family did mean more to her than she was prepared to admit.

'Just what are you up to, Miss Rosewall?' came a smooth voice somewhere above her, and Edwina sat up swiftly to find Damon Morven standing towering above her, his shadow completely blocking out the sun.

Edwina's first thought when she had recovered from the shock of his presence was of Peter, and how he never seemed to be around when he was needed. He was out, of course, on one of his fishing trips. 'I'm not "up to" anything,' she replied tersely.

'Oh, no? Then why the sudden transference of your allegiance from Knight to the Colonel? Did Knight put you up to it?' he demanded silkily.

'Peter had nothing to do with my working for the Colonel,' she replied frostily, thinking she couldn't even have a peaceful weekend without the annoying presence of this man. 'You're not going to believe me, but Peter and I are related. No doubt you'll check up on that, but you're going to be disappointed if you think you can prove otherwise,' she added furiously, as she got up, not liking being towered over.

'What work are you doing for the Colonel?' Damon demanded, 'I thought he'd decided to take things easy these days.'

'Why don't you ask him?' Edwina said angrily.

'In spite of what you think of me, I do have some competence. The Colonel's my employer, and as such I respect his privacy.'

'Paying you a good wage, is he?' Damon said dryly, and Edwina raised her arm to deliver a sharp rebuke, but he beat her to it. 'I'd have thought you'd have known better than to try that again,' he said casually, as his grip tightened on her wrist, making her wince.

'Demonstrating your strength again, Mr Morven?' she got out between clenched teeth.

His eyes flashed at this, and he suddenly released her. 'Odd how I always want to manhandle you, isn't it? he said silkily.

'Not really,' Edwina answered cuttingly, as she rubbed her sore wrist. 'You're not used to being at a disadvantage with a woman, are you? We're second class citizens to you. Stupid, I think you said, didn't you?' she added acidly.

A gleam of amusement came into his eyes as he stood back and surveyed her, and Edwina, conscious of his scrutiny, wished she had worn her shorts and T-shirt, rather than the skimpy sunsuit she was wearing. It was not as skimpy as the type Julia wore, but it was not exactly Victorian either, and she did not like the way Damon was taking his time in looking her over. 'Why don't you go and annoy someone else?' she demanded, beginning to feel embarrassed. 'I'm sure there must be a few more hotels you could buy up, or maybe an oil well or two,' she added sarcastically.

'Been checking up on me, have you?' Damon

asked blandly. 'The Colonel's no beggar either, but I'm sure you know that, don't you? Of course, he's a softer option, I'll grant you that. There's no fool like an old fool, but I hardly think he'd be stupid enough to commit himself even for a charmer like you,' he sneered.

Edwina's arm was half raised before she realised it. It was a purely instinctive action, but before he could react and catch it in another punishing hold, she dropped it to her side again, her hands clenched into fists.

Damon gave a low chuckle. 'You're beginning to catch on,' he said. 'Not so stupid after all, are you? At least not where self-preservation is concerned. Talking of oil, I now know who little Julia caught,' he went on smoothly, and Edwina looked quickly away from his mocking eyes before he saw how much that had upset her. 'Think he knows yet? Or is he still in the land of tinted spectacles?' he queried dryly.

Edwina whirled on him with blazing eyes. 'Just how low can you get?' she spat out at him. 'It's hardly the sort of thing one tells one's husband, is it?' she bit out, furiously angry with herself for her slip of the tongue earlier. 'But you wouldn't hesitate, would you? Not when you've more business to acquire. Nothing else matters, does it? Not even hurting a man as nice as Stanley. I told Julia she was mad, and she must have been,' she went on in a low voice, 'she must have had a brainstorm to want to—' Her voice petered out as she realised where this theme was leading, and turned abruptly away from him, so that he could not see the tears of frustration that had gathered in her eyes.

For a second time that morning her arm was caught and she was forced to come to a standstill, even though this time it was only a halting gesture rather than a hard grip, and she angrily shrugged it away. 'Go away,' she said in a low trembling voice, 'and don't ever push your company on me again!'

The hold imperceptibly tightened, still not a compelling hold but enough to prevent her from walking away from him. 'We don't seem to be hitting it off, do we?' said Damon, in what sounded like a slightly puzzled voice, as if he couldn't understand why she had taken that attitude.

Edwina turned slowly to face him, 'Look, I don't like you,' she said slowly. 'In fact, I think I hate you. If I can do anything—anything at all to stop you getting that marina, I believe I'd do it. The Colonel isn't such an old fool, you know, and you're going to need his help, aren't you? If you can count on anything it will be that I'm with the opposition!' she vowed furiously.

Damon studied her through narrowed eyes. 'So it's war, is it, Miss Rosewall?' he said in a low purring voice. 'So be it!' and he dropped his hold on her arm.

With no restraint to hold her now, Edwina marched away from him, not caring where she went as long as she was out of this man's vicinity, but she had not got very far before she heard his parting words addressed to her stiff back. 'Don't forget what I said about giving me a ring some time. You might need another sponsor before long, and I'm still interested.'

Edwina had no doubt as to what he meant by his last comment. He was not a man to mince his words. She was no good, but he was attracted to her, was what it all amounted to.

Tears of utter frustration coursed down her cheeks, as she glanced back quickly to see if he had gone, and a sigh of relief went through her when she saw that he had, so she went back to her lilo, where only a short time ago she had been relaxed and happy. Blast the wretched man! she thought angrily. Had he nothing better to do than to harass her? Well, he was under no illusion now if he had hoped to gain her help by subtle blackmail. It hadn't worked, and it never would.

She lay back on the lilo and closed her eyes, hoping for a peace that she knew would not come. Why on earth had she been so foolish as to bring up the subject of oil wells? He hadn't missed that, had he? It had given him the ideal opening to let her know that he knew who Julia had married, or, according to him, caught.

There was her relationship with Peter, too. She had blown the gaff there, and Peter had not wanted that brought out. He hadn't minded the Colonel knowing, but then the Colonel was not out to make trouble for him, not in the way Damon Morven would if he decided to get nasty.

Edwina drew in a ragged breath. She had handed him a weapon to use any time it pleased him. How could she have done a thing like that? she asked herself. Was it because she couldn't bear being labelled as a no-good gold-digger? Was it pride that had made her fling caution to the winds? She shook her head dumbly. The truth of the matter was that she did care what Damon Morven thought of her. If it had been any other man, then she wouldn't have cared a jot.

As he was attracted to her, so was she to him, but in a way that some poeple were fascinated by snakes, or spiders, a fascination that was compelling and yet repelling. In spite of the heat of the day, Edwina shivered.

At dinner that evening she told Peter about Damon's visit. She had to, because she had to tell him what she had told him, and that he now knew about their connection.

To her relief Peter was not at all put out. 'Doesn't matter,' he had said offhandedly. 'He'd have eventually have found out anyway, particularly if he'd have gone to the Colonel with any tittle-tattle in that line.'

Edwina shot Peter a quick surreptitious glance, but he was busy peeling a peach. So he had known what Damon Morven had thought of their association, she thought with a spurt of surprise, and she had thought—she swallowed. Like the Colonel, Peter was nobody's fool either. He was probably relieved that she had announced their true relationship.

'What is annoying is the way he always seems to turn up when I'm off the premises,' Peter said musingly. 'Almost as if he'd been tipped off,' he added darkly.

Edwina blinked. 'You mean he's got a spy in the hotel?' she asked.

He shrugged. 'Well, he tried to coerce you into sussing out the joint, I believe is what they call it, don't they?' he grinned, then quickly sobered. 'He does want that marina, you know.'

Edwina frowned. 'But that was different,' she said. 'He thought—well, still thinks, that I'm a scheming hussy. He surely wouldn't go to the trouble of planting someone here, would he?' she asked.

'He wouldn't need to,' Peter replied dryly. 'He's got so many business connections around here that there's sure to be someone who's related to someone else, if you know what I mean. Just a "keep your eye open" order would be enough, and a thank you in monetary terms later. They wouldn't look on it as spying, you know. All the same, I don't like it. I don't like it one bit,' he added angrily.

'Well, there'll be no more visits now, I can assure you,' Edwina said firmly. 'He wanted to know if you'd planted me on the Colonel to get him on our side.' She took a sip of her coffee. 'I denied it, of course, but that man only believes what he wants to believe,' she added dryly. 'The only thing that worries me is that he could make trouble for Julia, although I hope this wretched marina question will be settled by the time they get back,' she ended hopefully.

Peter swallowed the last of his coffee and put his cup down with a firm clink. 'That we can depend on,' he said grimly. 'They've got all the facts they need, and it's only a question of giving whoever's got the contract the go-ahead. There was no point in holding that second meeting, not when they all knew that Morven was asking for extra land, and unless I'm much mistaken it'll be as the Colonel said, this side of the project, that probably means the top of the bluff, next door to the Haven, in fact, and that it will be another of his fancy hotels.' He took a deep breath. 'There'll be pandemonium once such a plan is disclosed, but there'll be nothing we can do about it,' he added dismally.

'What will you do, Peter, if he does get the marina?' Edwina asked anxiously. 'Will you have to close down?'

Peter got up from the table. 'To be perfectly honest, I haven't really considered what I'll do. I'm putting off the evil moment, I suppose. Oh, I could keep it going as a hotel, I mean, but I would lose all my regulars, and it means starting again and working it up as a quiet hotel that offers nothing but a sea view, that's if I still have a sea view, for all I know he might decide to build a few fancy chalets on the beach.' He paused. 'The thing I shall hate most of all is losing all my friends, and they *are* my friends, you know. Most of them have been coming here for years for the game fishing, and I can't expect them to have to stand in a queue when the marina is built. No they'll book in there, of course, and probably pay me a courtesy visit in between times,' he ended with a wry attempt at a smile before he left Edwina.

Edwina stayed at the table and sat staring into space. She wished there was something that she could do for Peter. She thought of the Colonel, and shook her head. In spite of what she'd said to Damon Morven about going all out to influence the Colonel, she knew she would do no such thing. Colonel Melway knew Peter's predicament as well as Peter did, and he was a fair-minded man. She sighed. All they could do was hope.

The following Monday morning Edwina received an early telephone call, and for a moment she thought it was Julia, who rang at any time of the day, depending on her mood, and as she picked up the telephone, she presumed that Julia was going somewhere special that day and had been unable to contain herself from passing on the good news, but as she spoke her name, the smooth tones of the caller assured her that it was not who she thought it was calling her.

'Have dinner with me tonight, Miss Rosewall.' It was an order, and not a request, and as such Edwina was well aware of it.

'No, thank you, Mr Morven,' she said frigidly, in a very polite voice, wondering how long she was going to have to put up with this persecution.

There was a low chuckle on the other end of the line. 'So you recognised my voice,' he said, in a pleased-sounding voice. 'I'm off to New York in a day or so's time,' he added casually, too casually. 'I was wondering whether you had any message you'd like me to give your brother-in-law. No doubt I shall run into him at some time during the convention.'

Edwina's slim figure stiffened, and her hand holding the receiver went white as she tightened her hold on the instrument. 'Are you blackmailing me, Mr Morven?' she asked in a low fervent voice.

'Now why should I do that, Miss Rosewall?' he enquired blandly. 'It just so happens that I have a free evening, and I rather thought that it would be nice if you would consent to share it with me. Er—I have the penthouse suite here, you know. It has extensive views over the bay, and—well, after dinner on the balcony, I thought we could smooch to a few records—'

There was an appreciable silence after this, and Edwina drew in a shuddering breath that was not lost on the acute hearing of Damon. 'Was that a shiver of anticipation, Miss Rosewall,' he enquired silkily, 'or—?'

'Or, Mr Morven—definitely or!' Edwina managed to get out before slamming the receiver down hard.

She stood staring down at the now silent receiver resting in its cradle, and found she was trembling. He had said it was war, hadn't he? she thought dully. He must have known that she'd never have accepted such an invitation. He was giving her time to think about it, and she was sure he was convinced that before the day was through she would ring him back and agree to have dinner with him.

It was a 'be nice to me, Miss Rosewall, and maybe I won't upset the apple cart' proposal. But then she was supposed to be stupid, she thought scathingly, and if Damon thought he could railroad her into panicking as she had before, he had another think coming!

He'd have it all lined up—flowers on the table, a perfectly wonderful dinner, with plenty of pleasantries, if it stayed at pleasantries, she thought darkly, for she was well aware what he had in mind when he'd mentioned 'smooching' to records.

A shiver ran down her back at the very thought of such a happening, and what he would hope to be the finale of the evening. She could also imagine the outcome should she be such a fool as to fall for such a gambit. He would afterwards smilingly tell her that he had decided to put Stanley in the picture after all, and hadn't she been a fool in thinking otherwise. After which, she thought grimly, he would throw her out, with some such comment as to how he had enjoyed 'getting to know her better'.

Edwina's teeth clenched. She'd taken a lot from Julia in the past, but there was a limit, and she had just reached it!

At this point the receptionist, Miss Toomey, spoke to her. Her voice seemed to come from a distance, and Edwina blinked as she realised that she was only a few feet away from her, and telling her that the taxi that the Colonel arranged to call for her each morning to take her to work was at the entrance, and she nodded her thanks before snatching up her bag from the lobby table and going out of the hotel.

CHAPTER SEVEN

Edwina was still fuming when she reached The Dunes, the Colonel's house, nestling in a small cove on the east side of the Island, and with magnificent views over the east bay.

Her expression revealed her thoughts as she marched into the Colonel's study and threw her bag on to the desk allotted to her. 'Tell me,' she said to the Colonel who was at that moment perusing some papers on his desk and who had given a bright 'good morning, Edwina' on her arrival, 'what kind of jails do you have out here? I don't suppose there's one on the island, is there? They go to Nassau, don't they?' she asked grimly.

The Colonel blinked at the ferocity in her voice. 'Er—Nassau, my dear, but what you want to know a thing like that for is beyond my reasoning,' he added mildly.

'Do they hang murderers or give them a life sentence?' Edwina enquired earnestly, adding with tight lips, 'It would be worth it at that!'

The Colonel abandoned all interest in the papers on his desk. 'Who's upset you?' he asked. 'It's not like you to get worked up.'

Edwina walked round to her desk and sat down. 'I know,' she said wearily, 'but something about that man just gets me on the raw.' She took a deep

109

breath. 'I'm sorry,' she said, giving the Colonel a weak smile. 'He's only out to annoy me, and it's my own fault if he succeeds. There's nothing I can do about it anyway.' She pulled the typewriter towards her in a businesslike manner, to show the Colonel she was ready for work.

The Colonel's glance sharpened. 'Morven?' he asked.

Edwina nodded. 'As I said, he does it on purpose. I do wish that marina business was settled. He thinks I'm an undercover agent acting on Peter's behalf, you see,' she explained with an attempt at lightness.

'I'll have to have a word with him,' the Colonel said darkly. 'I'm not going to have you harassed like this. For goodness' sake, why didn't you say something before? I suppose he warned you to keep out of it, did he?' he asked.

Edwina pushed back a lock of hair that had fallen across her forehead. 'I didn't see why you should get involved,' she said quietly. 'It's a sort of private fight over—well, you know what,' she ended lamely, then added seriously, 'Look, I'm sorry I sounded off. It's just that sometimes it gets me down, and I'm sure that everything will settle down once he gets that contract—he will get it, won't he?' she asked the Colonel tiredly.

'I've a mind to put in a bid myself,' the Colonel said thoughtfully. 'There wouldn't be any quibbling then, I can assure you. That's why there's so much dithering on the decision. Yes, I'd say Morven stands a better chance. He's got the know-how and the cash, but it will cause a lot of bad feeling among the locals, of course. Not all of them, though, some will benefit—bound to, in the long run,' he added musingly. 'But if I—'

Edwina smiled weakly at him. 'You're supposed to be taking it easy, remember? What would you do with a huge project like that? I appreciate the thought, but I'd far rather you just concentrated on the book. Besides,' she added brightly, 'we've got to beat Chubby Charlie to it, haven't we? And you'll never do it if you start playing around with big business again, will you?' she scolded gently.

The Colonel grinned and raised his arm in a salute. 'Point taken,' he said appreciatively. 'No, by jove, we won't, will we?' and they got down to work.

There was a week of peace for Edwina after this little interlude—not that she was lulled into a false sense of security, for she was only too aware of Damon Morven's threats when trying to coerce her into having dinner with him, and at the back of her mind was the niggling worry of receiving a frantic phone call from Julia as a direct result of Morven's veiled threats being carried out.

On the following Monday morning, however, her mind was set at rest on that particular worry, for the Colonel, who had spent the previous week in an unusual amount of activity, out and about on various quests—unusual, because since Edwina had started working on the book with him, he was always at The Dunes, passed on a message that he said he had had from Damon Morven. 'Ran into him in town,' he said briefly, 'told me to tell you that he was sorry he was unable to pass on that message you'd given him to give your brother-in-law,' and he gave Edwina a bright blue stare. 'Gave him a message, did you?' he asked, plainly at a loss to understand why her deadly enemy should be passing on any kind of message.

Edwina's first reaction was puzzlement, then as realisation dawned, she gave a small sigh of relief. Damon was telling her that he had for the moment decided not to drop the sword of Damocles on her head. It was a reprieve, for the moment, anyway, until the project was settled, she presumed dryly.

'Oh, he told me that he was going to some conference,' she told the Colonel. 'He said he might run into Stanley, and asked if I had any message for him,' she ended lamely. 'It wasn't important,' she added earnestly, 'and as I've said, I don't like the man, so I just mentioned that he could give him my regards.'

Edwina hoped this satisfied the Colonel. To tell him the whole truth would have brought about a furious reaction and caused more trouble all round, and Edwina had had a week of peace and she wanted things left that way.

There was another reason, but Edwina refused to acknowledge it. She didn't want the Colonel to know, for purely personal reasons. She still hated the man, but he had his own code of honour, and he had let her off the hook, for a while at least. These were sentiments that she decided not to go too deeply into, for she could not understand why she should feel this way over a man who had continually harassed her. Maybe it was a sense of fairness, but whatever it was, she could not discuss it with the Colonel.

The following Saturday it seemed that Edwina's peace was at an end, for Damon Morven rang through to her at The Haven and invited her out to lunch. This time he gave her no chance of turning the invitation down, by a terse, 'I'm picking you up at twelve sharp,' order, and placing the receiver down at his end, leaving a bemused Edwina staring at the silent instrument in her hand, too surprised to be angry, and noting that she had only fifteen minutes' grace before he arrived.

If that wasn't typical of the man! she thought. Giving her just enough time to change into suitable wear, but not enough time to arrange for another appointment!

As she took a swift shower, she wondered what he had up his sleeve this time. It was possible that he had received the go-ahead for his marina scheme and wanted to pass on the good news that Peter was as good as out of business.

For once Edwina was pleased that Peter was not around. If her surmise was right, she would rather he heard the bad news from her than from a triumphant Damon Morven.

When she was dressed, she adjusted the white floppy bow of her blouse so that it overlapped the jacket of her navy blue two-piece, then stood back to examine the result, and was satisfied with her reflection. While she stared critically at herself in the mirror it suddenly occurred to her that not for one moment had she contemplated not accepting what had been more of an order than an invitation.

Perhaps she was stupid, she mused, but if it was news of the marina, then she was as much involved as anyone else. Good news for her, of course, if he had got that contract, but bad news for Peter. She sighed. You couldn't have it both ways, unfortunately. It meant peace for her where Damon Morven was concerned, and no retribution for Julia's stupidity, but on the other hand, Peter would have to rethink on the business front. Fortunately, moneywise, he was a comparatively rich man and had wisely invested his profits from the years of plenty, but Fishy was another story, and Edwina simply could not see him being allowed to hawk his wares on the select beaches of other hotels. There wouldn't be any point, anyway; all their food was provided for them by the hotels.

She sighed again as she placed the wide-brimmed navy blue picture hat on her head that went with the ensemble, and was in fact the outfit that she had worn at Julia's wedding, and collecting her shoulder bag, she went down to reception to await Damon's arrival, for it was just on the stroke of twelve.

There was no waiting, as Damon was there when she entered reception, and without a word he whisked her out of the hotel with his usual assertive manner and into his car, and then they were off at a speed that made Edwina wonder where the fire was, for he had hardly spoken a word to her, and his manner did not suggest a celebration, and she wondered a little belatedly whether she had been wise in allowing him to ride roughshod over her in this way.

The only comfort she had, as she stole a glance at his stony face as the car sped along the road, was that it was the middle of the day and she had his personal assurance that he did not ravish women until after eight in the evening!

The restaurant was the same one that the Colonel had taken her to a few weeks ago, and when they entered the dining room Edwina was ushered to the same table in the alcove that Damon had occupied on that other occasion, and she wondered if he had a share in the restaurant, because every other table was occupied, save for this one.

The way the waiter almost stood to attention while receiving their order confirmed Edwina's suspicion, and she ordered the same meal she had had with the Colonel. It saved time, for she was by now certain that whatever she ate she would not enjoy it, not with this grim-faced man seated opposite her, his cold grey eyes missing nothing.

For the life of her, Edwina could not understand why he had to take her out to lunch. By the look of his hard features, whatever he had on his mind could surely be aired either on the telephone or in one brief visit to her hotel, and she felt a surge of anger rise up at the way he treated her. Perhaps this was the only free time he had that day, and thought that he might as well have a working lunch, she thought furiously, and save a bit more of his precious time.

As soon as the waiter had been dispatched, he asked abruptly, 'What's your price, Miss Rosewall?'

Edwina had been idly looking around her at the chattering diners, and she jumped at the harshness of his voice. Then she blinked as she tried to make out what he was referring to. As she comprehended the question, she took a deep breath. He surely didn't mean—? and her wide lovely eyes showed her feelings.

'Stop looking so damned innocent!' he bit out at her. 'I'm through playing games with you. I asked you a question and I want an answer.'

'Perhaps you'd better rephrase the question, Mr Morven,' Edwina got out in a low furious voice that showed that she was through playing games too, and her hand went out to pick up her bag in preparation for leaving.

'You're not going anywhere,' Damon said silkily. 'I own this place. You wouldn't get past the doors once I gave the order to have you detained. You can try it, if you want, of course,' he said, giving her a wolfish smile that did not reach his eyes, 'but it will be very embarrassing for you. It's much friendlier this way, don't you think?' he added softly.

Edwina's hand left her bag, and she looked away from the mocking look in his eyes, as she silently conceded his victory. She had no doubt that what he had said was true, and she had been a fool to come.

Damon leant towards her. 'Look, I said I was through playing games, and I meant it. I don't know how you did it, and it's not often that I have to admit defeat. I want that contract, so I'll ask you again, what's your price for getting the Colonel to drop his bid?' he asked harshly.

Edwina stared at him, her lovely eyes blinking in her bemusement as she tried to come to terms with what he had just said.

'I only wish there were no witnesses around,' Damon said through clenched teeth. 'I know a sure way to take that cultivated wide-eyed look off your lovely face. Some other time, perhaps,' he added purposefully, 'because there will be another time, I can assure you,' he promised meaningly, 'no matter what the result.'

Edwina was still suffering from shock. So the Colonel had put in a bid, in spite of his implied concession to leave well alone and get on with the book. Her glance went back to Damon, who looked as if he was ready to chew nails. No wonder he was mad, she thought, and he was sure that it had been her who had put him up to it. She almost shivered. Talk about walking into the spider's web!

Damon did not miss the quickly dashed look of dismay on her face. 'Thought I wouldn't get to know about it until it was too late, did you?' he said softly. 'Well, I've got some friends in high places, too. I've heard of chivalry, of course, but this is madness on the Colonel's part. He's past managing a complex like this—why, dammit, he's retired! I take it all back about you being a stupid woman. You're a very clever woman—too clever, if I may say so, for your own good,' he purred menacingly. 'So let's get down to business. What do you want in exchange for getting the Colonel to back out?' he demanded.

Edwina took a deep breath. He was so certain that she held the key to his dilemma that it would never occur to him that she might not be able to make the Colonel back out. Even so, she was being given a golden chance to get this man out of her hair for good and all, and not only hers, she thought, as she began to realise the possibilities.

Her eyes, now narrowed in speculation, went slowly over the man who sat facing her with a sceptical look on his handsome features while he waited for her to name perhaps a hotel or two to be transferred to her name, or any other of his success-ful enterprises—why, she might even ask to be made a partner in the project itself! She blinked. The possibilities were endless, but best of all, she had this man at her mercy, and it was this last thought that was the most satisfactory of the lot! A small smile touched her lips. She was going to enjoy her lunch after all!

Their meal was served at this point, and gave Edwina more time to savour her position, but when the waiter left them, she knew she would have to make a start on her conditions.

'As a matter of fact, there are a few conditions that I'd want your word on,' she said brightly, as she helped herself to vegetables from the silver bowl beside her, and she did not miss the sneering look she received for this, but went on. 'Firstly,' she said, pushing her luck, 'I really don't see why you should want to build a marina anyway. I mean, you've got so much on hand elsewhere, haven't you? and I'd much rather you left our part of the island alone, however,' she went on hastily, seeing the dangerous glints in his grey eyes that told her she was running out of time if she continued on this theme, not to mention that she'd never be given the chance to name her conditions, not if she had correctly interpreted his look that said that he'd like to throttle her! 'Well,' she began, 'I want your word that you will not at any time make trouble for Mr and Mrs Nelson—and of course, that goes for me, too,' she added sweetly, her eyes registering the almost comical look of surprise on his face. That had been the last thing he thought she'd have on her mind with so much on offer, she thought with a twinge of amusement.

After his nod of confirmation, with a reservation that she decided not to pursue, for he had said plainly, 'No trouble for our dear Julia and Stanley,' but had forborne to add her to the list, but Edwina was not worried by this small omission, for it went without saying that once he had got that contract he was not likely to want to see her again, so she carried on. 'I also want your word that Peter Knight will be given access to that part of the beach that he has always used. I'm sorry if you had plans to put up some chalets, but that's out, I'm afraid. Oh, I nearly forgot,' she added, in consternation. 'There's a man called Fishy—I don't know his other name, but he sell crabs and things just below the hotel—on the beach, I mean. I want him to have the same access to the beach.'

She took a deep breath of satisfaction and leaned back in her chair, then took a sip of her wine. 'I think that's all,' she said happily, 'only we don't want a huge complex of buildings, and certainly not a casino,' she added sternly. Remembering what had been said about the Colonel liking a flutter, she couldn't have him sneaking off to play the tables when they were supposed to be getting on with the book.

For a short while Damon seemed bereft of speech, and his amazement showed on his face, as he queried innocently, 'Finished?'

Edwina nodded, then frowned. 'I'm trusting you to keep your word,' she said, giving him a wary look.

'Oh, I think I can comply with those conditions,' he said idly, then gave her a hard stare. 'You do realise that you could have set yourself up for life, don't you?' he asked dryly.

'I have all I require, thank you, Mr Morven,' Edwina replied primly, allowing a hint of amusement to enter her eyes.

'Having conceded to your demands, then,' Damon said smoothly, 'I now make one of my own. Dine with me tonight.'

Edwina's eyes lost all their amusement. 'You're already breaking one of the stipulations,' she said testily. It hadn't taken him long to revert to his old ways, she thought crossly.

'Er—which one is that?' he enquired innocently.

She glared at him. 'The very first,' she said, 'as you very well know.'

'Ah, but I agreed where Julia and Stanley were concerned. I said nothing, however, about you. I couldn't make a promise I didn't intend to keep, could I?' he stated airily. 'Besides, I fail to see why you're creating this fuss about a simple dinner date. It's a celebration, isn't it? I should get what I want, and you will get what you want,' he added blandly.

In the circumstances, and put like that, Edwina knew that it would be churlish to refuse, but she would have liked to have stuck to her guns, and she belatedly wished she had asked for a more personal stipulation to be added to the previous list, and judging from the mocking predatory gleam in his eyes, as she reluctantly agreed to have dinner with him, he was very well aware of what she had in mind.

The rest of the lunch went on smoothly, apart from a distinct feeling on Edwina's part that she had put her head in a noose! by the time the lunch was over and Damon had taken her back to the Haven, after casually mentioning that he would call for her at eight, Edwina found herself fervently hoping she would not be able to persuade the Colonel to drop his bid, or failing that, invite the Colonel to join in the dinner celebrations! There would be nothing that Damon could do about it, if, when he turned up at the Haven to pick Edwina up, the Colonel happened to be there, and Edwina just happened to invite him to join them, knowing how she felt about the man, the Colonel was not likely to let her down, she thought shrewdly.

Peter was just finishing his lunch when Edwina walked in, not that it appeared he had much appetite, she noticed, for he had only half finished his salad before abandoning it, and seeing his gloomy expression, she was half tempted to tell him his worries were over, or would be after she had seen the Colonel, for in spite of her wishful thinking, she was certain that once she had told the Colonel what had transpired between her and Damon Morven, he would be only too relieved to drop out of the competition.

When Peter had gone to his office to catch up on his accounts, Edwina took the opportunity to ring for a taxi to take her to The Dunes, and while she waited for its arrival, it occurred to her that Peter had been so immersed in his personal worries that he had not asked why she was not having lunch with him, which was most unlike him, so for his sake alone she had to go through with everything, even if it meant dining alone with that man.

On arrival at the Dunes, Edwina was pretty certain where she would find the Colonel at that time of day on a weekend, so she made a detour that skirted round the front of the house to the back lawns, and sure enough, there was the Colonel taking his ease in a low cane chair under the shade of a tree, with a long cold drink on a cane table beside him.

He saw Edwina as soon as she saw him, and waved a welcoming arm, shouting for his boy to fetch out another chair and a fruit juice for his visitor.

'Now, to what do I owe the pleasure of this impromptu visit?' the Colonel asked brightly, as Edwina settled herself in the cane chair the servant had brought out for her, and gratefully received the cold drink he had placed on the table within her reach.

'You've been holding out on me,' she said sternly. 'You've put in a bid for the marina, haven't you?' she accused him.

The Colonel looked suitably abashed, and took a sip of his drink, which Edwina suspected held more in it than just fruit juice.

'It's no use playing for time,' she continued in a schoolmarmish voice. 'You don't deny it, do you? Anyway, I know you have,' and she went on to explain how she had found out and all that had transpired between herself and Damon Morven, including the conditions she had imposed on him for getting the Colonel to change his mind, ending with, 'So you will back out now, won't you? I mean, there's no point now in your going through with it, is there? I've got what we want. He's going to leave Peter's part of the beach alone, and that probably means that he won't be asking for that extra piece of land.' She gave the Colonel an appealing look. 'So you will back out, won't you?' she repeated.

The Colonel scratched the tip of his nose, a habit of his when thinking, and seeing it, Edwina felt a spurt of alarm. Surely he wouldn't insist on going through with things now? she thought anxiously.

'Well,' he said slowly, 'there's no point. I mean, no reason to back out,' he amended quickly in an abashed manner. 'You see, I didn't exactly put a bid in. Er—you see—?' he ended lamely, looking like a small boy caught with his fingers in the jam.

Edwina shook her head bewilderedly. 'No, I don't see,' she said, and added indignantly, 'A man like Damon Morven doesn't get hold of the wrong end of the stick,' she said, now on surer ground. 'Did you put in a bid for the marina, or didn't you?' she demanded, determined to get to the bottom of things.

'Er—actually, no,' the Colonel replied. 'But I did put out a few hints in the right places, if you know what I mean,' he added quickly, seeing Edwina's growing impatience, for it was plain that she thought that he was just trying to get out from under.

'How could you sort of hint?' she demanded.

'Oh, it's easily done,' the Colonel said loftily, now looking relieved that it was out, and very pleased with himself. 'And by Jove, it worked, didn't it?' he added.

Edwina sat partially stunned. He hadn't put in a bid at all! Just casually mentioned that he was interested and intended to do so, and that was all it took! Rumour had then taken over, and before you knew it the word was around that it had actually happened! Edwina swallowed. If Damon Morven ever found out—She shuddered. It didn't bear thinking about!

It was plain that the Colonel thought she ought to congratulate him on a brilliant stroke, instead of looking as if she were contemplating joining the women's equivalent of the Foreign Legion!

'And I spent two hours at lunch with Damon Morven laying down the law on what he could do and what he couldn't do—for a rumour?' she almost wailed, going wide-eyed at the thought of her audacity. 'What,' she asked the Colonel, in an awed, hushed voice, 'will he do when he finds out? I suppose that didn't occur to you, did it?' she demanded accusingly.

The Colonel did not look at all repentant. 'No need for him to ever find out,' he said confidently. 'My name is not on that list of contenders. It never was, but no matter, he won't bother about anything like that once he gets that contract, and he has, you know. Heard it on the grapevine this morning. He'll be receiving confirmation early next week,' he added airily.

Preferably later, Edwina prayed, because she hadn't the Colonel's confidence. In the meantime she was due to dine with Damon Morven that evening, and just supposing—just supposing that some time that evening someone should ring and drop a little hint in his ear—? she swallowed.

'Don't know why you're worrying,' the Colonel said brightly. 'Turned out for the best, didn't it? Mind you, I didn't mean him to tackle you about it. Thought he'd make a beeline for me and try to do a deal, and I would have done precisely what you did—agreed on those same terms, I mean,' he assured her happily.

'In the meantime,' Edwina wailed, 'he's wrangled a dinner date with me! Called it a celebration, and I could hardly refuse, could I?' she added bitterly, and shot the Colonel an indignant glance. 'Well, you're coming with me,' she declared fervently. 'It was your brilliant brainwave that got us into this, remember?' she reminded him.

The Colonel coughed. 'Sorry, my dear, can't oblige. Got a chappie coming—to do with the book, you know,' he added hastily at Edwina's look of scepticism. 'He's over on holiday, only got a week or so here,' he added apologetically.

'Well, don't be surprised if I don't turn up on Monday,' Edwina said darkly. 'I don't know how long it takes a postcard to get here from the U.K., of course, but—'

The Colonel gave a short bark of laughter, that held a hint of surprise in it. 'I expected better things of you, Edwina,' he said, trying to adopt a stern attitude. 'Said you've nothing to worry about, and you haven't. You know you can count on me. Morven's all right—had a word with him. There'll be no hanky-panky, I can assure you. You go ahead and enjoy your dinner, you've earned it,' he added in a kindly manner.

At the Colonel's insistence, Edwina allowed him to run her back to the Haven, and several times repeated his assurance that all was well.

Edwina, however, remained unconvinced. Being a gentleman, the Colonel would never imagine that his calm assurance of there being no 'hanky-panky' could not be relied on, but then he had not witnessed the way Damon Morven had a nasty habit of 'manhandling' her, as Damon himself had put it.

CHAPTER EIGHT

Before the Colonel had left, he had warned Edwina to keep the news of who had been awarded the contract 'under wraps', as he had put it. 'Not supposed to know, you know,' he said in his abrupt manner of speaking. 'Tell Knight, of course. All on the q.t., though,' he had added, much to Edwina's relief, for she was not sure she could sit on such good news for even a day without saying something to put Peter's mind at rest.

'Was that the Colonel?' Peter asked her in surprise as they almost collided at the entrance to the hotel. 'You haven't started working weekends, have you?' he asked.

Edwina smiled. 'Oh, no, there was just something I had to see him about,' she replied, thinking that this was the part she was going to enjoy, and would give Peter no end of a fillip. His worries were over, but hers were just beginning. She frowned at the thought, and swiftly shrugged it away. Time enough to worry about that around eight that evening. 'I've got something to tell you,' she said. 'Let's go into the lounge,' she suggested, not wanting to take the chance of anyone overhearing what she had to tell Peter.

Mystified, Peter followed her through to their private lounge, and she told him all that had ensued from her lunch with Damon Morven.

He stared at her owlishly from behind his spectacles, obviously wanting to believe that his worries were over, but not as yet able to convince himself, since Edwina only gave him the bare bones of the story. 'Do you mean to tell me that Morven asked you to lunch to discuss this?' he demanded, then blinked in incomprehension. 'Why on earth should he do that? He's having you on,' he said indignantly.

Edwina shook her head. 'No, he wasn't,' she said impatiently. She had not envisaged having to convince Peter of his good fortune. 'He'd heard that the Colonel had put in a bid for the contract. Don't you see? He's always thought we were out to get the Colonel on our side, and of course we were, but we didn't put any pressure on him, did we? Anyway, he was certain that I was behind the whole thing and that the Colonel had only entered the contest for my sake. So—' she took a deep breath, 'he asked me out to lunch and sort of suggested we do a deal, providing I could get the Colonel to drop out.'

'You mean he tried to bribe you?' Peter asked indignantly.

'Well, I suppose, sort of,' Edwina mused, then grinned. 'He wasn't expecting any of the conditions I laid down—your free access to the beach, and no trouble for Julia. He was expecting to have to part with a block of apartments,' she said, and added with a wry twist of her soft mouth, 'you know, I think I slipped up there. He was so anxious to get that contract he wouldn't have quibbled. Anyway,

I got what I wanted, but I had to see the Colonel first.' Her face suddenly sobered, for she was back to her worries again. 'Would you believe it? The Colonel hadn't put in a bid at all, just threatened to do so, and gossip did the rest. He didn't have to back out. He was never in contention!' she finished.

Peter's face bore a beatific expression as he savoured this last point. 'The old devil!' he said admiringly. 'Told you he was nobody's fool, didn't I? Takes one to catch one, and Morven's got hoisted on his own petard,' and he gave Edwina a congratulatory pat on the shoulder. 'That was good thinking on your part, Edwina,' he said happily. 'So whichever way it goes, we've nothing to lose, have we?' he added in sheer relief.

She was not so sure about his last statement, but she sincerely hoped he was right, for she had no wish to spend the evening fighting for what was aptly named her 'honour'! However, she had no wish to spoil Peter's happiness. 'Well, no,' she said, with obvious reservations. 'But do keep mum about it. The Colonel obviously doesn't want the news to get around until the official decision is announced, but he does know that Morven has got the contract, and should be hearing some time next week.'

Peter came out of his pleasant reverie to give her a hasty nod of understanding. 'Oh, yes, of course I'll say nothing. Be damn hard, though,' he said with a grin. 'I want to shake everybody's hand. Martin's lost out, of course, but he won't mind half as much when he finds out that we've got our concessions, because if Morven keeps his word, he'll concentrate on the Star Point end and leave us well alone.'

'Er—I'm having dinner with him this evening,' Edwina said, trying to sound casual. 'He said we ought to celebrate,' she added. 'He was pretty certain he'd get the contract if the Colonel backed out, and of course he has. For goodness' sake, don't say anything to him when he comes to pick me up, will you?' she warned Peter.

Again she had Peter's assurance of not doing anything to 'rock the boat', as he cheerfully put it, and it occurred to Edwina that like the Colonel he had no worries about her entering the lion's den, and expressed the same sentiments, that she should enjoy herself, she had earned it.

Inevitably the time passed and reluctantly Edwina had to get ready for her dinner date with Damon. She was not certain what she ought to wear, but she was certain that they would be dining in his private suite, or penthouse, as he had loftily informed her. She was also sure he would do things in style, particularly if all she had heard about him was true, and he was accomplished in entertaining females. This last thought did nothing to reassure her as she searched through her wardrobe for a suitable dress.

It would, of course, have to be evening wear. Everyone dressed for dinner in the hotels, she thought, as she drew out a simple white cocktail dress with gold piping on the mandarin collar, and on the wide sleeves, and decided to settle for that dress, rather than her peach evening gown that was backless and had a deep V front. It would simply be asking for trouble if she wore that, she thought, as she recalled Damon's earlier suggestion that they 'smooched' to a few records after dinner.

Oh, dear! Why had she to keep thinking of things like that? What was wrong with her? The Colonel said he expected better things of her, but the Colonel didn't know the half of it, whispered a little voice at the back of her mind, that gave her no comfort at all!

When she was ready, she took a long deep breath before going through to reception to meet Damon. She had nothing to worry about, nothing at all— only—She swallowed, and squared her shoulders, then marched out of her room with the hardly helpful phrase of 'into the valley of death rode the six hundred' floating through her brain.

As before, there was no waiting, for Damon, resplendent in evening dress, stood chatting to Peter in the lobby, and a worried Edwina hoped that Peter would watch his words and not give anything away, and she could have sworn that he gave her a wink as she glanced back at him as Damon led her out of the hotel!

'I gather that the Colonel agreed,' Damon said to her, as they drove off from the Haven, making her cast him a quick wary look, wondering if Peter had said anything to him, but he interpreted the look correctly. 'I'm supposing that Knight knows, of course,' he added smoothly, 'and I did think he was more relaxed than when I'd last seen him.'

Edwina looked straight ahead of her. This man was clever, she thought, and knew that she had to be careful about what she said. 'The Colonel agreed not to oppose your application,' she said, and gave a light shrug. 'Peter was very worried, you know, and I saw no harm in passing on the news that all was well,' she gave Damon a quick glance before adding, 'as yet we do not know who will get the contract, but the Colonel thought the odds were on you,' she said, carefully selecting her words. Until notification was received, everything she had said was true, Edwina thought, and even grapevines occasionally got it wrong, she comforted herself.

Before long they were drawing up at the Splendour, and Edwina began to feel butterflies in her stomach, and wondered what the staff would think when they saw her in the company of the boss—but she needn't have worried, for Damon eased the big car round to the covered car park at the back of the hotel and from there they entered the lift that took them straight up to the penthouse.

This part of the hotel was unknown to Edwina, who had never gone above stairs when she had worked for the hotel, but had guessed at the luxury the suites would offer going by the bills presented at the end of the hotel stay.

As for the penthouse—her feet sank into the deep pile of the carpet that ran from the lift to the entrance to the suite, and only changed in pattern and colour in the actual living area. What spacious accommodation it was too, she thought, as she

stood hesitantly in the entrance to the suite, for it
might have been the hallway to a large house with
its own cloakroom, to which Damon casually suggested that she leave her wrap and then join him in
the lounge—the second door down the passage, he
told her, his eyes acknowledging her fervent wish to
get the evening over with.

After depositing her wrap, and taking a quick
glance in the lovely bevelled mirror that took up
half of the room space, Edwina could delay no
longer, and left the sanctuary of the powder room
to find the lounge.

In keeping with everything else she had so far
seen, the lounge was large and airy, and luxuriously
furnished, but she only gave a swift glance round
before moving forward to a well upholstered
cretonne-covered sofa, that Damon indicated that
she should relax on, while he fixed them an aperitif
from a small bar at the end of the room.

Edwina noticed that he had not asked her what
she would prefer to have, and she gave the glass he
handed her a distinctly wary look that brought
another of his mocking looks her way. 'Try it,' he
suggested smoothly. 'It's my own concoction.
Quite harmless, I assure you. I'm not offering you
more than one. I want you to enjoy your dinner.'

There was not much chance of that, Edwina
thought dourly, as she sipped her drink, but she had
to concede that it was pleasant and not too strong.

Damon watched her expression as she tasted the
drink with what she would have called an anxious
look, but she felt she must have been mistaken; this

man was too sure of himself to have any qualms about anything!

When she gave a little nod of acceptance that the drink was to her taste, he lifted his glass towards her in a salute. 'To starting again,' he said, his grey eyes meeting hers in an expression that puzzled her, and seeing that look of incomprehension, added, 'or to put it more plainly, here's to me and you getting better acquainted.'

Edwina's look of alarm produced a glint of amusement in his eyes, and this annoyed her. He was playing with her again, she thought, but she couldn't find the right words to express her thoughts, not without starting another war with him.

Damon carried his drink over to an easy chair opposite the sofa where she sat, and studied her while he took a sip of his drink, till she began to feel uncomfortable, wishing he would not look at her like that.

'Worried, Miss Rosewall?' he queried softly, adding, 'Edwina.'

'Of course not!' Edwina said stoutly, not at all liking the way he had said her name. It had almost been a caress. She was glad she was sitting down, in spite of her last firm statement.

'Well, you should be, you know,' Damon said silkily. 'I intend to see quite a lot of you from now on.'

Edwina started. He didn't believe in beating about the bush, did he? she thought indignantly, and gave him one of her old-fashioned looks. 'I told you once before that I'm not interested,' she said, hoping her voice sounded calm, but her heart was thumping.

Damon continued to study her. 'Aren't you?' he said blandly. 'I'll admit that you're terrified of me, and I intend to change all that. We didn't get off to a very good start, did we, but I mean to make up for that,' he added smoothly.

To Edwina's untold relief there was a tap on the door at this point, and at Damon's sharp 'Enter' command, a waiter wheeled in a trolley of food and took it out to the balcony where presumably they were dining.

When the waiter had left, Damon led Edwina out on to the spacious balcony where the table was set, with silver urns of food from where delicious smells were emitting to tempt the palate.

Nothing was said until Damon had served their starters, iced melon, and Edwina just sat uncomfortably and watched the proceedings. This was going to be ten times worse than she had imagined, she thought miserably. She had not expected an all-out attack, but more on the lines of sedate seduction, probably during the smooching session he no doubt had in mind after dinner was over. She had not imagined him calmly announcing that he was laying siege to her affections, because that was what he had meant, she was certain. She swallowed. If he was hoping to allay her fears where his intentions were concerned, then he hadn't chosen the right way to go about it. She was more afraid of him now than she had been before!

When the melon was disposed of, they started on the rainbow trout, and a bemused Edwina watched Damon expertly remove the skin off his portion. She had to admit that it looked and smelt delicious. He couldn't have known it, of course, but this dish was a favourite of hers, and even in these restricted circumstances, she ought to be able to put up a good showing on the culinary front, if not on any other.

'What will you do when the Colonel's book is finished?' Damon asked her suddenly, making her start in surprise, for this was something she really had not thought about.

'You know about the book?' she said, astounded because the Colonel was not one to talk about his private affairs.

Damon nodded, and reached for his wine. 'Gave it as an excuse for not attending a shareholders' meeting a while ago. He was sadly missed. He usually chairs the meetings. He might be retired, but he's got his fingers on the right financial buttons. So?' he persisted. 'What are you going to do when the book's finished?'

Edwina took a sip of her wine. 'I really haven't thought about it,' she said slowly, and added quickly, 'time enough for that when it happens.'

Damon's grey eyes met hers over his glass. 'Well, I shall need a secretary for the project,' he said. 'You'll be on the spot then, won't you? You can keep me in line, as it were,' he added with a spark of amusement in his eyes.

Edwina took another hasty sip of her wine, and it

caught in her throat and made her cough, and, amused, Damon handed her a glass of water. 'See what I mean about you being terrified of me?' he said dryly. 'I offer you a job, and see what happens!'

She threw him a look of annoyance. He ought not to have rubbed that in quite so baldly, she thought indignantly, but said nothing. She only knew that she could not work in close proximity with this man. No matter what, she must not be bulldozed into accepting his offer. Her dilemma was how to refuse without offending him.

Damon's eyes watched the changing expressions in her lovely eyes that unknown to Edwina told him all he wanted to know. 'Look,' he said blandly, 'I'm not asking for an answer now. I'm asking you to think about it, that's all. As you said, there's no rush,' he concluded smoothly.

That was what he said, but she got the distinct impression that what he really meant was that he was a patient man up to a point, but don't go beyond that point. He had made up his mind on one salient fact where she was concerned, she was not going to be allowed to walk out of his life, not until he gave the word, that was.

These thoughts shook Edwina, but she was certain that she had read the situation correctly, and if there was anything she did not want it was to get emotionally involved with another man. She had not enjoyed her last encounter in the romantic stakes, and was not the type to enjoy a flirtation. Her large wide eyes that so plainly showed her thoughts stared out at the twinkling lights of the harbour just below them, and above them count-less stars shone in a dark blue velvet sky. A time-old sadness entered Edwina's heart, and she wanted to weep. Her slim hand still holding her wine glass tightened perceptibly on its slender stem as she made the effort to control her feelings.

'Want to tell me about it?' Damon asked softly, breaking into her unhappy reverie.

Edwina blinked, and stared at him as if she didn't know what he was talking about, but she knew he wouldn't be fobbed off by such a ruse. He would go on probing, and she could not explain how she felt, not to him, for somehow he was inexplicably in-volved in the emotional trauma she had just experi-enced, and she didn't really understand it herself.

'I suppose,' she said slowly, after a lengthy silence, 'that I'm homesick. Odd, how it can sud-denly catch up with you, isn't it?' she went on determinedly, her mind casting about for a let-out, and then Philip came to mind and she saw a way out of her difficulties. 'You see, I can't take another job,' she said casually. 'I was hoping to persuade my fiancé to come out here, but I don't seem to be having much luck, so in all probability I shall have to go back home.'

Once it was out, she felt terrible. She was not normally a liar, and when she attacked her Crêpe Suzette it tasted like leather in her mouth—and it served her right, she told herself, but there had been something in Damon's voice when he had asked her if she wanted a shoulder to cry on—which was what he had meant, that had sent the alarm bells ringing out loud and clear again, and she decided she would far rather have been on the receiving end of his temper than receiving comfort from him. Anger she could cope with, kindliness she couldn't.

Damon's eyes were hooded as he contemplated her trying to look totally immersed in the enjoyment of her sweet, then he touched his lips with his napkin and threw it down. 'Are you telling me you're engaged?' he demanded.

Edwina lost all interest, or all pretended interest in food, and laid her dessert fork down and pushed the plate away from her with an emphatic nod. 'Yes,' she said, adding a little indignantly, 'I don't see why you're so surprised.'

Damon's mouth twisted cynically. 'And he agreed to let you come all the way out here without him?' he queried sceptically.

Edwina had an answer to that. She had never thought she would be grateful for Julia's indiscretion, but at that moment it was a blessing. She picked up her wine glass and finished the little she had left, and shook her head when Damon attempted to refill her glass. 'It was through Julia, really,' she explained. 'She suddenly decided she wanted to travel, and as we had connections out here,' she took a deep breath, 'you know we—well, my family, lived in Nassau until I was seven, and then went back to the U.K. My father was attached to the Consulate, you see.' Edwina felt she was beginning to flounder, so she hastened on to the next part. 'My mother didn't like the idea of Julia going on her own, and I thought it might be nice to see the Caribbean again, so I agreed to come with her,' she ended lamely, darting a quick glance at Damon, who was watching her closely—too closely.

'And after she married?' Damon queried in a purring tone, that plainly said that he thought she was mistaken if she thought he was falling for that.

Edwina swallowed. This wasn't going to be so easy. 'I had to stay and see that all was well,' she said defensively. 'I—well, you know what Julia's like,' she added, not missing the way his firm lips straightened. 'Not,' she went on hastily, 'that she's a bad girl, just thoughtless, and I had to be certain she would settle down, and of course, as I said, I was hoping to persuade Philip to come out here,' she lied stoically.

'What does this Philip do?' asked Damon, and Edwina was gratified that at least he did believe in his existence.

'He's a dentist,' she replied.

'He also appears to be somewhat of a fool,' Damon said harshly. 'I'm damned if I'd let my woman go careering off into the blue, wayward sister or no wayward sister!'

Edwina looked suitably indignant, but deep down she was immensely relieved. Damon was back to the angry stage, and she preferred things that way. She decided to pour more fuel on the smouldering ashes. 'I think that's unfair,' she protested. 'You know nothing about him. I thought it was pretty good of him to agree to the trip,' she declared.

Damon's harsh bark of derision told her she had succeeded in keeping things going nicely, and she got up suddenly from the table. 'Well, thank you for the dinner—it was splendid,' she said brightly, but firmly, in the tone of voice that plainly said that she did not intend to put up with any more disparaging remarks where her fiancé was concerned, and without more ado she walked towards the lounge with the intention of collecting her wrap and being on her way—only things did not quite work out that way.

She had got as far as the lounge when, as once before, Damon beat her to the door and stood blocking her way, and she could tell from his eyes that he was good and angry—no, furious, she thought with a twinge of anxiety, but she did not expect what happened next, for she was suddenly pulled into his arms, surprise taking her unawares and as she stared up at him and was about to protest, she found herself being kissed in a way even her ex-fiancé had never kissed her.

When he finally let her go, she was outraged, not to say stunned, and her lips felt as if they had been pounded by a pumice stone, for there had been no gentleness in his treatment of her; it was a punishment, and a sheer imposing of his will on hers, but there were tears in her eyes as she stared back at him.

Damon's breath was coming fast as he met her look. 'I've wanted to do that for a long time,' he said coldly. 'Now that I've got it out of my system you can rest easy. It wasn't exactly a trip to the heights, was it?' he sneered. 'I guess you and that milksop of a fiancé of yours are well suited!'

Edwina whirled away from him and hurried to collect her wrap. She didn't care how she got home, all she knew was that she was going, and she would not bother about the lift either, the stairs must be somewhere, she thought wildly, as she headed for the front door of the suite.

To her fury, Damon stood waiting for her at the front door and he opened it as she reached it. Edwina went straight on out without a glance at him and her head held high, but she was forced to follow him to the lift, then she saw the stairs. 'Thank you,' she said icily. 'I prefer to walk,' and froze as his hand caught her arm.

'Don't be a fool!' he snapped harshly. 'Do you know how far up we are?' he demanded.

She flung his restraining hand off her arm. 'I don't care!' she said wildly. 'I said I'm walking!' and she spun away from him.

She had only got a few yards when she was swung bodily off her feet and placed over his shoulder, and with her fists angrily pounding his back she demanded to be put down, but to no avail, and she was unceremoniously carried to the lift where she was dumped down in much the same way as he might have dumped a sack of coal, and an outraged Edwina glared at his back as he closed the lift doors and pressed the down switch, then leaned back against the door panel to face her, while he casually took out his cigarette case and lit a cigarette.

'One of these days,' he warned her, 'you'll do as I say, when I say.' He drew deeply on his cigarette. 'Okay, so you're booked. I might do a lot of things, but I draw the line at filching another guy's girl, especially when he's not around to stake his claim. You can consider yourself lucky that you got out in one piece,' he added harshly, as the lift arrived at the garage, and Edwina was hustled out towards his car. She did not need any help in getting in, and sat as far away from him as was possible on her side of the seat.

Not another word was said. When they reached the Haven, Edwina tore open the car door and was out in a flash, and without a backward glance fled into the sanctuary of the Haven.

It was a long time since she had cried herself to sleep, but she did that night, after passing through several stages of emotions that ranged from righteous indignation to white-hot rage in which she fondly imagined her tormenter to be at her mercy and about to be boiled in oil!

Peter would have been extremely alarmed had he witnessed any of these emotional traumas, but true to his usual custom, he was in the bar swapping yarns with his friends and had no idea what time Edwina got back.

By the time she had got to her shower, she was a little more calm, but as the force of the water jetted on her face and touched her sore lips and made her wince, she thought angrily that it was a pity that he hadn't remembered his code of honour before forcing his kiss on her—and a brutal one it had been, she thought, going back to the furiously angry stage. He might just as well have beaten her!

The trouble was that he was frustrated, she thought pithily. He had got the seduction scene all planned out. He'd done it plenty of times before, no doubt, and had probably got it down to a fine art by now, she told herself, only it hadn't worked this time.

It was almost funny, she thought, as the tears started raining down her face. Tomorrow, she would be able to laugh about it, but somehow tonight . . .

CHAPTER NINE

NOT surprisingly, Edwina awoke with a headache the following morning, and almost winced at Peter's goodhumoured remarks at breakfast, but after he had given her a quick assessing look, he obviously decided that she had rather overdone the celebrating the previous evening, and was feeling rather delicate, so he wisely kept his thoughts to himself.

Monday could not come soon enough for Edwina, who needed something to do to take her mind off her misery. The laughter that she had promised herself that would come on the morrow had never come, instead she felt a yearning chasm of aching intensity spring up inside her, and she could not understand these feelings, since they were totally alien to her.

As Damon had so baldly pointed out, she had been lucky. She could by now have been another of his women, absolutely enslaved and dreading the day when he threw her out of his life. As it was, she still had her pride, and was still, as he had aptly put it, 'in one piece'.

Back at work on the book, Edwina threw herself into feverish activity, and the weeks flew by, and soon they were on the homeward run, and the highly satisfied Colonel said that it was about time that they saw the publisher, an old friend of his who had jumped at the chance of handling the publication.

Even if Peter was so caught up with his own affairs that were going so nicely, and hadn't noticed Edwina's total lack of spontaneity, and her long silences, the Colonel had, and had remarked upon it on several occasions. He was worried that the book was taking too much out of her, and there was no need for her to work so hard, particularly after receiving her last report from home that had contained the news that Sir Charles Taylor had gone down with gout, and an end had been put to his memoirs for some considerable time.

Edwina managed to allay the Colonel's suspicions that there was anything wrong with her by somehow dredging up a bright answer to the effect that she enjoyed the work, and naturally wanted to see it finished, although she suspected that he was not entirely convinced that there was nothing else wrong. But he did not press the matter.

In the meantime, Damon had got the marina contract and work had begun. All this she heard from Peter, and of course, the Colonel, who was taking an avid interest in the whole project.

She also knew that Damon was keeping Peter well primed on each stage of the development, occasionally sending him blueprints, and a much gratified Peter had sung Damon's praises, and what a good job he was doing, only Edwina knew that it was not for Peter's sake that Damon was keeping them informed, it was to let her know that he was keeping to his side of the bargain. This she knew for a certainty; she also knew that he hadn't bothered to call in at the Haven to deliver these missives, even though he must constantly be within a short distance of the hotel.

At last the day came when the book was ready for the publisher, and the Colonel decided they had both earned a holiday and suggested a week in Nassau. 'Kill two birds with one stone,' he had said happily. 'I've promised to attend a conference there, and we can push this in to the publisher, and be on hand should he want any alteration. Do you good, you know. I won't be wanting much done, and you can take a look around your old haunts. Er—Miss Pinkerton's gone over to the head teacher, I'm afraid,' he said with twinkling eyes, 'but I daresay you can find plenty of things to do.'

Edwina did not really want to go to Nassau. Now that the book was finished, she had her future to see about, and could see nothing for it but to go back to the U.K. She could hardly stay after what she had told Damon, and in a way it was better that she did go.

All her unhappiness was now centred on this balmy island, and a certain impossible man who had made life so difficult for her, but whom she could now admit she loved with a yearning she had never known before. It was not difficult to get news of him, because his name seemed to be on every-one's lips, Peter's and the Colonel's, to mention but a few, and all rapidly changing their previous views of him. 'A good man.' 'Don't know what we were worrying about, he's making a good job of the marina.' 'Just what we wanted,' and so on.

There were times when she castigated herself for being a fool and turning down the only chance of happiness she had been given, but this thinking did not last long. A vision of Julia would arise in front of her, like a ghoul from the past, and with it would come Damon's expression when she had mentioned her sister's name that night. Without knowing it, it must have been that knowledge that had been at the back of her mind when she had had that inexplicable feeling of sadness as she had looked over the harbour that night, and Damon had sensed that sadness, but she couldn't have told him what it was, even if she had known.

There were no daydreams for her of a happy ending. Better to accept the knowledge that she was one of the unfortunates who always chose the wrong man. There was also the underlying sadness that being the kind of man Damon was, he was not likely to bow out of the picture, not if he were really serious. He was a man who knew what he wanted and would move mountains to gain his prize, and it was this salient fact that effectively stopped Edwina dwelling in the land of makebelieve.

The weekend before they were due to leave for Nassau, she decided to tell the Colonel she would not be taking up his offer of a holiday, but Julia rang through with the news that they would be home on the Wednesday, and hadn't she a lot to tell Edwina, and just wait until she saw the clothes she had bought in New York. While she rambled on,

Edwina's heart sank. She was unhappy enough without having the cause of her unhappiness parading her furs or what have you in the self-satisfied manner that was purely Julia. No matter how fond of her she was, Edwina simply could not stand that, not at this time, and before she had thought things out she found herself explaining that she was off to Nassau with the Colonel for a week's holiday. The book was finished, etc.; almost babbling in her anxiety to get out from under.

Julia was most put out. As usual she thought of no one else but Julia, and she crossly commented that surely the trip to Nassau could be put off, and then she could go with Edwina, she needed to get some of her tan back—but Edwina would have none of that and explained that it was not exactly a holiday, and that the Colonel would be attending a conference, and she would have to take notes for him, underlining how busy she would be. Maybe they could take a week off together another time, she said vaguely; only there wouldn't be another time, she vowed as she put the phone down on a definitely sulking Julia. When the Nassau trip was over, she was heading for the U.K.!

A day later the Colonel and Edwina booked into the Consul in Nassau, a very old establishment that must have been running in Queen Victoria's time. The Colonel had remarked that it was old-fashioned, but efficient in an old-worldly way. No tourist venue was this hotel, for it did not cater for them, but drew its clientele from the ranks of the Consulate and their acquaintances, and all other applications were strictly vetted. If you could mention the right names for references then you were admitted, if not, the uniformed desk clerk would cheerfully direct you to another hotel.

As Edwina took stock of the spacious reception area that held an aura of silence not unlike that of the reading room in a public library, she thought of the Splendour and its milling tourists, the shouted laughter of the carefree residents as they hailed their friends while they waited to be taken out on some expedition or other, and she had to smile at the thought that such goings on would be considered outlandish in this hallowed atmosphere. She even wondered if a string quartet would be playing during the tea interval!

When she had got her key, she made straight for her room, while the Colonel made a foray into the lounge to seek out old friends who he knew to be staying in the hotel for the conference he was attending, telling Edwina he would meet her for lunch around midday.

It was a very warm day, and the first thing Edwina wanted was a cool shower, and she sincerely hoped that although the hotel had not moved into the twentieth century as far as decorations went, for there were no chrome fittings here, that they had installed bathroom facilities in the room accommodation.

As the lift drew to a whispered halt on her floor and she stepped out, she saw a few cases standing just outside the lift, that apparently the porters had not got around to delivering to their respective destinations, and noting that hers and the Colonel's were among them, she collected her case and took it with her to find her room, smiling, as an amusing anecdote the Colonel had come out with during their journey that morning, came to her. He had been describing the hotel and saying that fancy décors were all very well, but there were times when they were a positive menace. There was one occasion, he told her, where most of the hotel that he was staying in consisted of glass-fronted monstrosities, every entrance was plate glass, and he had walked into one of them. 'Felt no end of a fool, you know,' he had declared. 'Damn near sued 'em!'

The corridor was a long one, and Edwina began to wish she had waited for the porter to deliver her case, for womanlike, she had packed far more than she actually needed, but she hadn't been sure that she could rely on the Colonel's promise to let her make her own entertainment. He was just as likely to drag her in on some dinner party or other occasion that required more than the ordinary sundress appearance, so she had come prepared.

On noting the numbers as she passed along, she saw she was nearing her goal when she got to the two-sixties, for her number was two-sixty-six, and as she glanced up at a door which she very nearly passed, she saw the number at the same moment as the door opened and a chambermaid emerged with towels over her arm, and with a sigh of relief Edwina put down her case, answering the chambermaid's murmured comment of how warm it was, and went through to her room.

The room was strictly in keeping with the rest of the hotel, and there were no concessions here of modern décor either, but entirely adequate for its purpose. Edwina was pleased to note that her hopes as far as bathroom facilities were concerned had been fulfilled, for just off an area that had been cordoned off for luggage was a mini-bathroom complete with shower unit.

She placed her case on the bed and started to unpack her toilet things, placing her room key with its large numbered ring that she had not had to use on to the dressing table before she lost it in the unpacking, and for the first time she began to feel as if she might enjoy her holiday after all.

It had been hard going on the way to Nassau, with the Colonel continually chatting about this and that, and Edwina had longed for an interlude. As fond of the Colonel as she undoubtedly was, she longed for some peace, and to be able to get down to working out how soon she could make her arrangements for her journey back to the U.K.

She had kept this knowledge entirely to herself. Not even Peter knew what she had in mind, for as before, he would attempt to persuade her to stay, and that went for the Colonel, too. He would not be fobbed off on any homesickness excuse, and would demand to hear the whole of it, and that was something that Edwina could not divulge.

No, she thought, as she picked up her toilet bag and went to take her shower, the best way was to tell no one about her plans until it was too late for anyone to do anything about it. They could come and see her off at the airport if they wished, she would allow them maybe an hour's grace for that, but only that.

The shower was cool and refreshing and she had no complaints there, but she did need a larger bath towel than the one provided, she thought, as she wrapped the inadequately sized towelling round her, and that only just covered the bare essentials, and wandered out to the bedroom to dress.

She took her time in searching out a cool dress to wear, shaking out a linen favourite of hers and laying it out on the bed. She had plenty of time, so there was no hurry, she thought lazily, resolutely pushing away her earlier miserable musings, determined to enjoy what would be her last week in the Caribbean, and she was just in the act of removing her towel when she heard a sound that made her freeze into immobility. Someone had inserted a key in the lock of her door. They had obviously not looked properly at the numbers, but she relaxed as the thought came to her that the key would not fit, and whoever it was would soon realise their mistake.

The next moment she was staring at Damon, who looked as startled as she did, his grey eyes slightly widening as they took their time in looking her over, then his features hardened, and he said softly, 'I suppose you know what you're doing?' as he advanced into the room.

Edwina found her voice. 'Get out!' she gasped, clutching the bathtowel closer to her bare frame.

'I rather think that's my line,' Damon remarked,

still in that soft insinuating voice. 'This is my room, you know, and I'm not one to turn down an invitation, not where you're concerned,' he added meaningly. 'I really shall have to do something about the way you girls insist on sharing my bedroom,' he threatened, as he walked purposely towards her.

Edwina stood petrified. Only half of what he had hinted got through to her, but she would think about that later, she thought wildly—right now she had more pressing things on her mind! 'Please, Damon,' she whispered, moving back against the dressing-table, which was as far as she could go from him. 'It can't be your room. My key's over here,' she nodded frantically towards the top of the dressing table. 'Look at it. This is number two-sixty-six.'

It was the first time that she had used his Christian name, although she hadn't realised it, but Damon had, and it pleased him and, had she but known it, gave her the respite she so badly needed. 'Used the key to get in, did you?' he asked casually, his eyes monitoring her every move.

Edwina blinked. 'Er—no,' she said. 'I didn't have to. The chambermaid was just leaving as I got here,' then her eyes showed their consternation as she had a nasty thought. Damon had used his key, and it had fitted! She spoke her thoughts aloud in a hushed whisper. 'But your key fitted, didn't it? So I've obviously got the wrong room.' She clutched the towel tighter to her. 'I do apologise, Mr Morven. If you would just give me time to—'

'You called me Damon before,' Damon said, cutting into her request.

Edwina stared at him. Had she? Then she flushed on meeting his mocking eyes.

'Go on,' he ordered. 'Say it again.'

She looked away from his knowing eyes. 'Please, Damon,' she swallowed, 'would you give me time to get dressed,' she said in a low voice, and stole a look at him, then almost wept in relief to see that he was smiling, and no longer angry. Then his expression hardened. 'Go and get dressed!' he bit out at her.

She needed no second bidding, and pounced on her case and took it to the bathroom with her.

A few minutes later she was dressed, and when she returned to the bedroom she saw that Damon was still there. She had half hoped that he would make himself scarce, but he had obviously chosen to stay, and was seated on a chair by the window, looking up at her as she entered the room.

One part of her saw the tired lines around his eyes. She knew every inch of his features as well as she knew her own. 'You've been working too hard,' she said gently. 'You're tired.'

Damon's mouth hardened, and for a moment she thought he hadn't heard what she had said, for he seemed miles away, then his eyes met hers and he said harshly, 'Get!' and threw her key at her.

Edwina stiffened but managed to keep her features wooden as she complied with his order. This was probably the last memory of him that she would have to take back with her to England, she thought wildly, and had an hysterical urge to laugh, as she firmly closed the door behind her. He was so polite!

As she moved away from the door, she heard a distinct click, and looked back at the door, thinking that he had locked it, in case she decided to go back for an encore, but she was wrong, for it was the number digit that had moved, and now swung like a pendulum, the nine becoming a six! 'Thank you for nothing!' she whispered fiercely, sending the offending digit a baleful glare before looking for her correct number.

Safely inside her room, she sat down shakily on the bed. If anyone had told her that such a thing could have happened, she would have totally disbelieved them.

The worst of it was that she was sure Damon thought she had taken a leaf out of Julia's book, and had panicked at the last moment. No wonder he had told her to 'Get' in that abrupt manner.

Her hands were trembling badly, and she clenched them together in an effort to stop their spasmodic jerks. It would have been embarrassing enough for whoever it was who had booked that room, but it had to be him, hadn't it? she thought bitterly. What had she done to deserve all this? she wondered miserably.

She got up from the bed. She couldn't possibly stay here now, she thought wildly, as she paced the confined space of the bedroom, and she couldn't tell the Colonel why, either!

Her brow creased in anguished thought. If only

she could come up with some excuse as to why she had to leave the hotel! If only she knew someone in Nassau that she could use as an excuse for changing hotels. Someone on holiday, perhaps? Could she suddenly meet someone she knew from back home and spend the rest of the week with them in their hotel? She could arrange to meet the Colonel for the visit to the publishers, couldn't she?

Cold sane reasoning, however, soon put a stop to these speculations. How could she say she had met an old friend when they had only just arrived? And she knew no one in Nassau, certainly not from the Consulate days, it was all too long ago.

With a sinking heart she knew she would have to see it through. Her only consolation was that the convention was of a short duration, for two days only, and she must somehow hope to keep out of Damon's way. The Colonel had said nothing about taking her to the convention, just mentioning the publishers, so with a little bit of the luck that seemed so far to have deserted her, she thought she ought to be able to cope until Damon returned to the out-islands.

The time that Edwina was dreading came all too quickly, and she went down to the lounge to meet the Colonel, who had had the foresight to stand close to the door of the lounge to wait for her, and this was just as well for Edwina, because the place was crowded with people getting in pre-lunch appetisers, and you could hardly hear yourself talk for the general chatter and folk welcoming each other.

The Colonel settled Edwina at a small table near

the bar, so far ignored because it only seated two, and most of the crowd stood around in the middle of the large bar lounge and gradually spilled out, making it almost a scrum to get to the bar. She noted how popular the Colonel was and how a way through was made for him in deferential respect, and the many times he would give either a quick nod of recognition, or hold a hand up in greeting when he spotted people he was acquainted with.

Soon he was back with a sherry for Edwina, and something a little stronger for himself, and while the Colonel had a word with an oldish man who had stopped by their table, Edwina cast a surreptitious look around for Damon, dreading seeing him, but even more worried that he should see them and come and join them.

Then she saw him at the end of the lounge, near the door to the dining room, with a group of people, one of whom was a well dressed, lovely woman, who appeared to be scolding him about something in a coquettish way. No doubt because of his recent absence from the social scene, Edwina thought, for the marina project occupied a lot of his time, but she was sure he would make up for lost time once that was finished, particularly where the women were concerned, she thought miserably.

From where she sat, and where Damon stood, there was the whole space of the room between them, and with Damon's back to her that made him unaware of her presence, she felt she could relax, since it was certain he would be in the dining room long before they got there, so there was no possibility of him joining them for lunch, another worry that Edwina toyed with earlier, for the Colonel was apt to throw out such an invitation should he see Damon.

At that moment the Colonel spotted an old friend of his, a frail-looking old man seated by the window across the room from where they sat. 'Edwina, would you mind if I had a word with an old friend of mine?' he asked. 'I won't be long,' he promised before he left her.

Left to herself, Edwina felt her eyes go back to Damon as if drawn by a magnet, and she could see that he was still being entertained by the woman, and she wondered who she was. She was certainly not a secretary, those white hands of hers that she gesticulated so frequently with, with their heavy load of expensive jewellery, and the long painted fingernails, was sufficient proof of this. Whatever else she did, she had never pounded a typewriter. She was probably a high-powered executive's daughter.

Edwina was so intent on her musings that she did not notice that a man had stopped to speak to her, and when her bemused eyes met the brown merry eyes of a fair-haired, young-looking man, she gave a start, feeling she had been caught out unawares, exposing her inner feelings where Damon was concerned, but a moment's reflection soon quelled this unpalatable thought, since the man was a stranger to her and couldn't possibly know of her connection with Damon.

'Hallo, you're new, aren't you?' the man said

brightly. 'Saw you were with the Colonel,' and without asking permission, he sat down in the Colonel's seat. 'I pride myself on knowing who's who, and what's what,' he went on. 'Oh, I'm Jeremy Day, by the way.' He lifted an expressive eyebrow at Edwina, and she complied with her name, in a half amused, half surprised manner, thinking that on closer study, the man wasn't all that young, and had a rather rakish air about him. 'So,' he went on, 'how is it you're with the Colonel? He's no relations as far as I know. And don't,' he added, giving her a knowing look, 'tell me you're his secretary. He hasn't got one.'

Edwina was just about to put him straight on that when a voice she knew well said smoothly, 'Careful how you treat the lady, she's engaged,' and she found herself staring up at Damon, who at that moment was not looking at her but at Jeremy Day, in a manner that puzzled her, for it was not what one might call friendly, and his voice too, had held a definite warning in it.

The man's reaction was odd, too, she thought, as he got up slowly, made some confused remark about no offence meant, and moved away.

Edwina was not generally slow on the uptake, but she did feel she had missed a line somewhere, and she was about to demand what that was all about from Damon, and who did he think he was, and what right had he to interfere with what had seemed a perfectly innocuous conversation, when Damon turned on his heel and left her seething.

The more she thought about it, the more convinced she was that she had the answer. He hadn't been able to take the fact that someone else might succeed where he had failed. The man was probably an accomplished flirt, she thought angrily; perhaps he had scored over Damon before. As if she couldn't handle that kind of man! she fumed silently.

The Colonel joined her then, apologising for being away longer than he intended. 'Saw Day arrive,' he said, 'but couldn't get away. Couldn't leave the General in the middle of a sentence. Still, glad Morven coped. The man's a menace! Sound enough in business, but got a shady reputation where the ladies are concerned,' he said abruptly.

Edwina wanted to cry. If the Colonel was worried for her, then the man must have been a very dubious character indeed. But how had Damon known he was at her table? The room was full of people, and his vision obscured, not to mention the fact that he had had his back to her. Lastly, and not least, why had he bothered? When she recalled his harsh 'Get!' to her only a short while ago, it didn't make sense. Perhaps he thought she was as mixed up as Julia was, and needed to be saved from herself, and she was all the more certain that he was sure that her nerve had failed her when he had found her in his room, but the intention had been there, all the same.

After a perfectly miserable lunch, during which Edwina did her best to respond to the Colonel's bantering chatter, she was relieved when he spoke of taking a nap in his room, and that as the conference was due to start at three, he would be fully occupied, and suggested that she took herself off on whatever pleasure she had in mind.

She had almost broke out into hysterical laughter at this suggestion. She was so unhappy, she simply could not envisage going anywhere, and certainly not for pleasure. The only thing she could be sure of was that she would not run into Damon, for he would be at the conference, and the way she felt, she never wanted to see him again. He was a positive jinx where she was concerned, and she couldn't wait to get out of his line of fire.

It was home for her, and the sooner the better, she thought absently, as she stared at the imposing statue of Queen Victoria in front of the Law Courts on her walk about Nassau.

It was odd, really, how little she remembered of her earlier life there. For instance, she must have passed this statue many times on her way to Miss Pinkerton's seminary, always accompanied by a young nursemaid, but it had evidently left no impression upon her. In all probability, she mused, she had been worrying about the coming lessons, for Miss Pinkerton had been a tartar, and had drummed in correct behaviour and woe betide anyone who stepped out of line.

Even now, after all those years, Edwina could hear those stentorian tones. 'You are young ladies, and you will act accordingly!'

Edwina thought of Julia, and what a pity that she had not had the benefit of such training, for surely—? She sighed. What was the use of thinking like that? What was done was done, and there was no going back. At least Julia was happy. Even though she didn't deserve Stanley, she had got him, and all that she required in her code of happiness which meant money and the resulting luxury that money could buy.

As Edwina turned away from her preoccupation with the statue, she felt incredibly lonely, although all around her tourists were milling, photographs were being taken of the statue with the Law Courts behind it, and of the policeman standing on his box in the middle of the road, in his quaint Island uniform that smacked of Colonial days, and delighted the tourists. All this she saw, but she was not part of it.

She passed a dress boutique and saw a silk scarf that she thought she might buy for her mother, because she would soon have to think about gifts to take back with her, but she was so depressed she put that off for another day. Tomorrow perhaps, when things didn't look so bleak, she thought, and continued on her wanderings, wishing she had not to go back to the hotel for dinner, but could get herself a meal in one of the small cafés, where no one knew her, and she would not have to put up a front of gay bravado on how much she was enjoying her holiday.

She could cope with this, but what she could not cope with was seeing Damon again, and this time being unable to avoid being in his company, his all too knowing eyes watching her and thinking . . .

CHAPTER TEN

EDWINA's fears of seeing Damon again that week turned out to be groundless. He was not present at dinner that evening, and after searching in vain for his tall powerful frame, for had he been anywhere in that large crowded dining room, she would have seen him, the same sixth sense that apparently worked with him, worked with her, too, and she could sense his presence no matter where he was in the room.

After her first inward sigh of relief, she was perversely disappointed, and she remembered the lovely woman he had been talking to at the pre-lunch gathering, who, she felt certain, was either entertaining Damon at dinner, or he was entertaining her.

He was not present the next day at breakfast, and Edwina thought he had either had an early breakfast or—but she preferred not to think about that.

As this was the last day of the conference, she knew he would be making tracks back to the out-islands, presumably straight after the Conference ended, and when he did not appear for lunch she realised that her worries over meeting him again were over.

Now that she could relax, she had to admit to a feeling of disappointment that he had chosen to keep out of her way—at least that was her first thought, but on deeper reflection she realised that a man as popular as he was would have many calls on his time, and it was nothing to do with a vain hope of hers that he would think it would be embarrassing for her if he stuck around. She knew him too well for that. As far as he was concerned, she was an irritating woman who couldn't make up her mind whether or not to embark on an affair with him, and when the chips were down, hadn't been able to see it through.

Thoughts like these tempted her to stay in the Caribbean. She wouldn't have to worry about running into him, even though he was working only a few miles from the Haven, and had been for several weeks. Edwina had seen nothing of him, and the recent events at the hotel had done nothing to alter this state of affairs, except make it that much more certain that he would keep his distance.

There would still be the problem of finding herself a job, but perhaps she could do what Julia had done, and search elsewhere for a job, here in Nassau, perhaps?

So went her thinking while she wandered around Nassau. She still had plenty of free time on her hands. They had been to the publishers', and much to the Colonel's annoyance, the editor had insisted on certain items being expounded on events that the Colonel had taken care to play down, and for which he had an impressive array of decorations. But he couldn't fool the editor, who for one thing knew him too well, and for another, knew a little more about the desert campaign than the Colonel had given him credit for!

At that time there was a battle of wills going on, and at the Colonel's explosive, 'Damn it all, it's my autobiography, isn't it?' to which the editor had replied meaningly, 'Precisely.'

As the matter was a particularly embarrassing one for the Colonel, Edwina was excused attendance at these meetings while they thrashed it out, but she thought the editor would win in the end. As he had so rightly pointed out, either it was an autobiogprahy or it wasn't an autobiography. If it went out as memoirs, then it would soon be seen that the Colonel had a particularly bad memory for certain heroic events!

While Edwina wandered around, paying visits to the Botanical Gardens, and from there on to the Cactus Gardens, seeing but not really taking in the bright tropical flowers of reds, pinks, mauves, of oleanders and hibiscus, and the glorious purple passion flowers. The numerous stalls where straw hats were piled up, all silk-embroidered with the bright motifs of the island flowers. Shopping bags, handbags, all beautifully decorated with bright silks, spilled over on to the sunlit paths, and behind the stalls sat the industrious natives of the islands, still at work on creating more goods for sale.

There was none of the wonder of the first-time tourist visit to the island for Edwina, even though she could remember little of her earlier stay there, but the constant cries of 'Oh, look at that flower! What a beautiful colour!' that would come from the visitors as they strolled through the flower markets, or caught sight of a brilliant red hibiscus, that trailed over balconies of the graceful wooden-structured Georgian-style houses, picturesque in their own right, and as old as they looked, made her realise that she must have absorbed more of the island's floral beauties than she was aware of.

But all the time the inward struggle was going on inside her mind, to stay or not to stay. She would not have much time to make up her mind once she got back to the out-islands, and there would be all kinds of diversions placed in her path. Julia, for one, she thought dryly, not to mention the treachery of her own heart that might succumb to any temptation offered to stay within distance of Damon.

By the time the holiday was over, and Edwina was on the way back to the out-islands with the Colonel, she had made up her mind, and this time there was going to be no backsliding, for she had her return flight ticket tucked in her handbag and would leave precisely a week after their return.

Back at the Haven, she rang Julia up and told her she would be over to see her the next morning, and once that was done she felt that she could relax. Peter had been surprisingly pleased to have her back, and for the first time it occurred to her that in spite of his preferred state of bachelorhood, he was lonely, and just the fact that one of his own kin was around gave him pleasure.

This, she realised, was just one of the little temptations she would be presented with before she went, but she was determined to stick to her guns. Peter had managed very well before they arrived, hadn't he? she told herself sternly, feeling mean at keeping her departure quiet until the last moment.

The same thing would happen with Julia, she was sure, but again, she was letting nothing, but nothing, stand in her way. It was her life, after all was said and done, and now that she had made up her mind to go, the thought of home shores became increasingly dear to her. It was a kind of homesickness, and she felt a longing for her father's company, and his dry sense of humour that somehow put everything into perspective, and soon, she was sure, she would be looking back on this episode of her life with a kind of wonder, as to how she could have been such a fool as to daydream over a man like Damon Morven, and she would no doubt marvel over the narrow escape she had had, considering the piratical nature of the man.

It was all happening just as she thought it would, Edwina thought dryly, as Julia hurried to greet her the next morning, in a most unlike Julia way, and flung her arms around her big sister, in a manner that suggested that she knew that she was going, and she would never see her again, but as Edwina knew that she could not possibly know, she felt that it was just the machinations of fate, having one last go at her, and she was having none of it.

She was, however, a bit concerned over Julia's appearance, for she had seemed to have gone a bit slimmer, and her complexion was paler than usual.

Of course, she would not have had much sun at that time in New York, so that would account for it, she thought, and in all probability she had lived it up too much, with too many late nights and goodness knows how many cocktail parties.

She talked too fast, too, even for Julia, Edwina thought, as she listened to her account of what she had done, who she had met, and what clothes she had bought, and lugged out a fabulous full-length fur for Edwina to admire, and by this time Edwina was beginning to get really worried, and the frightening prospect of drugs reared its ugly head. Julia was definitely not right, but Edwina couldn't put her finger on what was wrong, and when Julia, in the middle of replacing the fur in the wardrobe, suddenly closed her eyes and held on to the wardrobe door to steady herself, Edwina hurried over to her and got her to a chair, making her put her head between her knees to prevent the faint.

When she had partially recovered, Edwina got her a glass of water and sat watching her with anxious eyes as she slowly sipped it. 'You've been overdoing it, haven't you?' she said accusingly, but her heart was pulsating in fear of what was really the trouble. If anyone could stand any amount of late nights, Julia could, so it had to be something else. Perhaps she had picked up a fever or some other distressing disease on her travels, Edwina thought worriedly. There was no thought of going home now, not if Julia was ill.

To her utter consternation, Julia giggled and choked on her last sip of water. 'Don't blame me, blame Stanley,' she said, with a brave attempt at raillery.

Edwina stared at her. 'Because he took you to New York, you mean?' she asked anxiously.

Julia handed her the glass and gave her an exasperated look. 'Look,' she said, 'I know Mother wasn't very good at this sort of thing, explaining about the birds and bees, I mean—'

Edwina gasped, and her eyes widened. She had got there at last! 'You're having a baby?' she asked incredulously, still not able to grasp this momentous occasion. Julia with a baby was something else!

Julia ought to have looked very pleased with herself, but at that moment she burst into tears. 'Yes, and I'm terrified!' she wailed. 'I know babies are born every second in the world, but this is me, and I'm frightened to death at the prospect,' she added tearfully, and clutched at Edwina. 'Stanley's worse than I am. It was all I could do to get him to leave me for a morning, so I could tell you about it. He thinks I ought to go into hospital straight away!'

Edwina couldn't help smiling at this. She could well imagine the way Stanley would fuss over her, but she was still suffering from shock.

'Look,' said Julia, determinedly blowing her nose, 'you'll have to have a word with him and tell him to stop fussing. He's over the moon, of course, and hasn't really come down to earth yet, but he's got to stop putting cushions behind my back each time I sit down, and insist that I put my feet up, or I'll go mad! I don't know what I'd do if you weren't here. Can you imagine Mother?' she added with a sniff. 'If it wasn't for you, she'd be on the next plane out, and I'd have two of them sending me up the wall. She'll be over for the birth, that's certain, but at least I can keep her at bay until then,' she ended.

Up until then the news of the baby had entirely pushed all Edwina's well laid plans out of her mind, but now she had to come to terms with the fact that she had no choice in the matter, she had to stay with Julia. It wouldn't be a matter of weeks either, but nearer a year before she could contemplate leaving.

'You can't,' went on Julia, unknowingly cementing Edwina's thoughts, 'think what it would be like if you weren't around. Stanley's first thought, when he'd recovered, was that I should go and stay with his mother in New Orleans, and I should absolutely hate that. Not that I don't get on with her, I do, but she's very old-fashioned, you know. I wouldn't be able to sneak a cigarette or a Martini when I fancied one—she's very much against what she calls "unnatural behaviour". So I got all indignant when Stanley suggested it, and asked if he'd forgotten that I had a sister and if anyone was going to be around it was you, and he didn't argue then. He wasn't thinking properly, he said, and of course I'd want you to be with me. Not all the time, of course,' she added hastily, 'but later on, when—' she gave a loud sniff. 'And to think I bought all those lovely clothes in New York, and now I have to go into sacks!' she complained.

Edwina spent most of the day with Julia, comforting, and being in turns, amused and exasperated, by her sister's emotions, but as the news had only been confirmed that week by her doctor, Edwina thought that, like Stanley, Julia was still in shock, and would settle down given a week or two to recover.

She was also able to have a word with Stanley when he took her back to the Haven, about not fussing too much over Julia, and giving her a breathing space by taking up his normal pastime of game fishing, and promising to keep an eye on Julia for him. She also reminded him to make sure that Julia wrote to their mother, for her sister was not a good correspondent and was probably hoping that Edwina would pass on the news for her, but this had to come from Julia herself.

Back at the Haven, Edwina spent the time before dinner taking a well earned break, and only after she had really assimilated the fact that Julia was going to have a baby did she review her own position.

There was absolutely no possibility whatsoever of her going home now, not until after the baby was born, and as Julia had prophesied, her mother would by then have joined them, and probably her father, too. Edwina sighed. Could she go back with them? she wondered, and thought of her mother's reaction to this plan, and how she would lecture her on her thoughtlessness in thinking of leaving Julia with no kith or kin to turn to should she need help. So it was definitely no go.

The only answer was to get herself a job as soon

as she could, she told herself, and preferably else-where, returning to her earlier idea of working perhaps in Nassau, telling herself that she would start first thing in the morning, as she went to join Peter for dinner.

Peter took the news with the same reaction as Edwina had and exclaimed, 'Julia with a baby? It's mind-boggling, isn't it?' which more or less echoed Edwina's thoughts on the matter. She also agreed with his dark comment of, 'I should buck up and find yourself a job, Edwina, or you'll land up as a permanent fixture at Kingfishers. I don't suppose the Colonel has anything else on offer now that the book's finished, has he?' he asked.

Edwina shook her head. 'No,' she said, 'but I think he's working on it. He told me not to do anything rash, but to wait and see what turns up. He's probably sounding out a few of his executive friends,' she added—but when the Colonel had said that to her, he did not know that she was planning to leave that weekend, and she had not been able to tell him.

'There might be something for you down at the marina,' Peter said thoughtfully.

'I don't fancy that,' Edwina said quickly. 'I thought of trying my luck elsewhere, say around Nassau,' she added.

He frowned. 'Julia won't like that, and I don't think I like it either. I'd much rather you were here.'

They didn't know, they couldn't know why she wanted to move away, Edwina thought desperately, and for all she knew the Colonel might have a word with Damon hoping to get her a job on the project, and she hated to think what might result from such a request. Had fate not stepped in and prevented her from leaving, it wouldn't have mattered, but now it did matter, it mattered a lot, and she was back to the worrying stage, and even contemplated ringing up the Colonel to prevent such a happening. She could sort of hint that she had her eye on a job in Nassau, she thought distractedly.

The more she thought about it, the more convinced she became that that was exactly what the Colonel would do, and she couldn't wait for the following morning when she could be off on her quest. It didn't have to be Nassau, she told herself, but Nassau would be the place to go initially to see what jobs were going. However, she said nothing to Peter at breakfast the next morning, waiting until he was off on another fishing trip before setting off, growing more impatient as the time ticked away and Peter took his time in going.

It was nearly eleven before she could leave the hotel, and to her consternation she came face to face with yet another blockage in her path, this time in the formidable frame of Damon Morven, and there was no pretending that she hadn't seen him, because they met at the door of the hotel, and seeing his grim features as they alighted on her, Edwina was convinced that her worst fears had been realised, and the Colonel had approached him about a job for Edwina—and here he was, she thought frantically, about to enjoy telling her why he had turned the Colonel's request down.

Terrified that the not unnaturally curious Miss Toomey would have a front seat at her denouncement, Edwina whirled on her heel and went back to Peter's private office, with Damon hard on her heels, and she had the certain feeling that should she try any fancy moves, such as trying to shake him off, she would be backing a loser.

This was proved by the way he shut the door firmly behind him and stood in front of it like an avenging spirit gathering forces for the final blow in the conflict, and Edwina was trying to find some defence to ward off the attack.

'You little liar!' Damon muttered between clenched teeth, his eyes narrowed to slits as he surveyed her.

Edwina's first thought was that he had just learnt of the Colonel's non-existent bid. She knew she was in trouble up to her neck, but she had no defence against that accusation, and looked hastily away from him, for she could imagine his absolute fury at the way he had been deluded.

'Your engagement was broken off before you left England,' Damon went on in a hard tight voice. 'I knew you were scared of me, but I didn't think you'd go to those lengths to keep your distance. All that drivel about waiting for Philip to join you! I could wring your lovely neck for that. Do you realise the hell I've been through these past months?' he shouted at her. 'You might at least have the courage of your convictions, floating around my bedroom with only a towel on,' he fumed. 'And why the hell I didn't settle things for once and for all, right there and then, I'll never know!'

Edwina swallowed. That had been the last thing she thought he'd find out about, and from his point of view she supposed it was bad enough. It had given her a way out of the seduction scene he had planned. In a way she was relieved; he was only mad because he had lost out on what was probably one of his most successful manoeuvres.

'And that's not all,' he went on in a soft purring tone. 'There's the little matter of the Colonel's bid.'

Edwina sat up at that, jerked out of her whimsical musings, and her wide eyes met his.

He nodded grimly. 'Thought I wouldn't hear about that, didn't you?' he said softly. 'Well, I kept my side of the bargain, didn't I? You've still to keep yours, and this time without a fictional fiancé—got that?' He glared at her. 'You can't have it both ways,' he said harshly. 'Either you want me around or you don't, but I'll tell you this much, if I'd known then what I know now, your Lady Godiva act would have had a different ending. I'm through playing games with you, so you'd better make up your mind, and be careful what you say, because you're going to have to stand by it, no matter what. Okay, so you took a toss back there in the U.K., and that was the real reason why you joined your sister on her travels, wasn't it? And I didn't need a crystal ball to read between the lines, our little Julia didn't have to spell it out,' he added grimly.

Edwina gasped. 'You saw Julia?' she asked worriedly, thinking that Julia was in no state to be bullied.

Damon took a deep breath and met her glance with a trace of irony in his grey eyes. 'I wasn't going to get the truth out of you, so I sought it elsewhere,' he said abruptly, and before she could remonstrate with this, he went on in a hard voice. 'You've got till tonight to make up your mind. I'll be back at seven, and don't try ducking out on me, because I'll rout you out no matter where you are, got that?' He opened the door. 'Between now and then you'd better do some hard thinking,' he warned her, 'but just remember that you owe me. If it's still no go, then that's fine by me, and final!' Then he was gone, leaving a gasping Edwina to collect her scattered wits.

When her heartbeats had subsided to a more regular beat, she went carefully over everything that he had said, and nowhere in between his threats and furious accusations, had he given a clue to his feelings, apart from 'did she want him around.' She closed her eyes. He wanted an affair with her, she thought miserably, and she had known that all along, and was the reason why she had kept her distance from him. It wasn't so much that she was frightened of him, as that she was frightened of the consequences of such an alliance.

Nothing had changed, except that Damon felt that he had been short-changed by her lies about being engaged, and it was as well for her that he hadn't found out about that before she did what he called her 'Lady Godiva act' in his room, she thought hysterically, and what he had promised would have been the result of that little episode would surely have become fact.

Edwina felt like taking a slow boat to China. Julia would just have to cope on her own. It was a case of every man for himself—or in her case, every woman! When you had to go, you had to go!

The phone rang at that precise moment, and she stared at it in frozen immobility, certain that it was Damon, then common sense prevailed. It could hardly be him, he had only just left her.

It was Julia. 'You'll never guess who came to see me this morning,' she said coyly.

'Damon Morven,' Edwina said flatly, spoiling Julia's surprise.

'Well?' Julia said impatiently.

'Well, what?' Edwina replied, still in a flat unenthusiastic voice.

'I'm going to scream!' said Julia, in a high-pitched voice. 'For heaven's sake, the man's crazy about you! What happened?'

'I know,' Edwina said dully. 'As for what happened, nothing did. You see, I can't make up my mind whether to have an affair with him or not. It appears I have until this evening to make up my mind.'

She heard Julia take a deep breath, and wondered if she was about to faint again. 'Look, you're mad if you pass up this chance. Do you know how many women are gasping for that man's company? And you've got it all wrong. He's on the level. He doesn't have affairs. You can take it from me—I know. I heard enough about him at the hotel.' Then Julia sighed loudly. 'Why do I have to have an idiot for a sister?' she complained.

Edwina thought that was rich, considering who had got her into this mess in the first place, and she cut the conversation short by promising to keep Julia informed.

All right, she thought wearily, as she put the phone down. Let him come, at least she would be safe in the hotel with Peter within shouting distance if things got rough, for not for one minute did she believe that Damon would just walk away when she said 'no go', not when he thought that she owed him. In a sense he was right, she thought tiredly, but his price was too high.

As for Julia's assertion that he wasn't a man to have affairs, she didn't believe that either. If he had been serious about her, then he would not have been so harsh about it, would he? Not asked her if she wanted him around—for goodness' sake, what kind of a proposal was that?

Edwina tried to fill in the rest of the day by keeping herself busy, doing odd jobs and writing to her mother, not, of course, mentioning Julia's news, but just keeping her up to date, her father as well, by telling him all about the publisher's editor's remarks re the Colonel's book, and she knew he would utter a sigh of envy at the speed at which the book had been compiled while Sir Charles's lengthy epic was still in its infancy.

By the time Damon was due to put in an appearance, Edwina had herself well in hand, having gone through several rehearsals of what she was going to say to him after she had delivered her final answer, just in case Damon had any other ideas.

She had told Peter that he was dropping in that evening, adding that she thought he was going to offer her a job, which was not so very far off the mark, she had thought ironically as she had said this, but it had satisfied Peter, who had said he would be in the bar, and when things were fixed up, why not bring Morven through to the bar for a drink? Edwina had thought this was hardly likely, as they would not be parting on amicable terms considering that she was not taking the job!

As usual, Damon was punctual, and Edwina, seeing that he was in evening dress, thought he must have another appointment after he had seen her, so she was not too pleased at his abrupt, 'Ready?' giving the yellow linen suit that she was wearing, and had not bothered to change out of since that morning, a look that suggested she might have changed for their date.

Edwina caught the look and its meaning, and flushed. 'I hadn't planned on going anywhere,' she said firmly.

Damon's lips thinned. 'We're having dinner at my place,' he said. 'I should have thought you would have realised that.'

She was ready for a fight. 'How could I?' she retorted angrily. 'You only said you were calling back to see me.'

Damon ignored her anger and glanced at his

watch. 'I've fixed dinner for eight-thirty,' he said calmly. 'There's plenty of time for you to change. I'll go through to the bar and have a word with Knight while I'm waiting,' and left the utterly confounded Edwina staring after him.

Now what did she do? Her teeth caught her lower lip as she debated this latest dilemma that Damon had landed her in. How did you cope with a man like that? Ought she to wander through to the bar and say something like 'I've decided not to accept the job,' to Damon? There would be nothing he could do about it, not with Peter on the spot. After which, she told herself, following through with this hypothetical situation, Damon would murmur something about there being no reason why she should not have dinner with him. He had probably already told Peter he was taking her to dinner.

One of these days she would provide herself with a white flag, Edwina thought despondently, and have it handy ready to wave it each time Damon won a round! Then she pulled herself up sharply. What was she thinking of? After this evening, it would be all over.

All over, whispered a small voice inside her, and she felt the wetness gathering at the back of her eyes, but she knew what she was going to do, and went through to her bedroom to change.

This time there was no hesitation on her choice of dress, and the peach it was, with its bare back and low V-frontage. If Julia was wrong, she wouldn't have to worry about the birth, she thought darkly;

she just wouldn't be around!

When she was ready, she drew a deep breath and stared at herself in the dressing-table mirror. There was no doubt that the dress suited her, and for a moment her courage almost failed her, but she determinedly picked up her wrap and gathered up her evening bag, and taking another deep breath, went to find Damon.

Damon's eyes registered his approval at her transformation, and Peter gave her a look not unlike one that her father might have given her in pure paternal pride, and as Damon laid a possessive hand on her arm in preparation for leaving, Peter said in a teasing voice, 'I won't wait up for you,' that clearly showed that Damon had his full approval for keeping her out all night!

As Damon guided her to his car, Edwina wondered how they could all be so blind. All it took was a sought-after man, and not only sought after, but a very rich one, too, and add the fact that he was a bachelor, and he got the go-ahead all round, she thought scathingly.

Eventually, they arrived at the penthouse, with Damon, as before, not bothering about small talk, but concentrating on his driving during the journey, only Edwina was not entirely convinced of this, and thought he was probably working out new moves, as the last ones had proved a failure. She put her wrap in the cloakroom and went to join him in the lounge, where again, as before, he was mixing their drinks. It was like a re-run of the previous scene, she thought, as she accepted her drink from him, and devoutly hoped for the same ending!

There were echoes again from the last time, when he held up his glass in a salutory gesture, only this time the words were different. 'To us,' he said quietly, but his eyes said much more.

Considering that she had not given him the answer yet, Edwina thought that was typical of him. He thought he knew it!

'I'm not sure about the toast,' she said, her lovely eyes meeting his, 'but here's to a pleasant evening, anyway.'

Damon's expressive brows lifted at this, and he put his glass down in a decisive action that made her cling on to hers, just in case he had decided to liven things up a bit—but she needn't have bothered, for he calmly took the glass away from her, surprising her with his action before she could do anything about it, and the next moment she was on the receiving end of a close, almost suffocating embrace, and her protests were cut short by a heart-stopping kiss, after which she was too breathless to complain, and certainly too weak to make the effort.

'That's better,' Damon said softly, his lips roaming her temple as she leaned weakly against him. 'Why the devil you have to put up such a front beats me. I know you've got it as bad as I have, and I don't make mistakes, not over anything like this,' he murmured, as his lips sought hungrily for hers again.

By this time Edwina was past caring. She didn't

want him to let her go. She didn't want his lips to leave hers, and again came that sensation of coming home. She belonged to this man. She had known it all along, and maybe tomorrow she would be able to think straight, but not now, with his lips on hers.

When he did release her, Edwina tried to collect herself. She was sure her hair was a mess, and she felt incredibly gauche. She was not used to this sort of scene. It didn't matter when she was in his arms, but now, when she was expected to make small talk while they waited for their dinner, she couldn't think of anything to say, and came out shakily with, 'And I haven't given you your answer yet.'

Damon grinned wickedly. 'Haven't you?' he said. 'Well, perhaps we'd better start again,' and he made to take her in his arms, but Edwina moved away from him, causing him to raise an eyebrow.

Away from his touch, she began to think properly again. Enough to realise that she had to get a hold on herself, or she was sunk, and that meant keeping her distance, and she wondered miserably when dinner was going to be served, and a swift glance at her watch told her there was another half an hour to go, and somehow—

'Hungry?' asked Damon, managing to inject a suggestion in his voice that had nothing to do with food, and underlining it with, 'So am I.'

Edwina pretended she hadn't heard that, and cast about desperately in her mind for some other subject, and Julia came to mind. 'You shouldn't have gone and bullied Julia,' she said, glad to have something to accuse him of.

'Who said I bullied her?' Damon asked innocently. 'I'll admit she had a fright when she knew
who was calling on her, but she was very co-oper-
ative when she realised I hadn't gone there to start
making trouble for her.' His eyes swept possess-
ively over Edwina, and it was almost a caress, as if
he had kissed her, she thought weakly. 'The little
devil had the effrontery to flutter her eyelashes at
me,' Damon said dryly, 'but I soon put a stop to any
of that nonsense,' he added firmly, as he picked up
his drink and took a sip. 'You know,' he said
thoughtfully, 'it's as well for her that she's married
to a nice guy. No sister-in-law of mine is going to
behave like that again,' he said darkly.

Edwina, who had followed his example and
taken a sip from her Martini, suddenly coughed.
She had forgotten to swallow, his last words had
floored her.

Damon watched her as she hastily put the glass
down. 'Now what?' he asked. 'It's not as strong as
all that.'

'I—' Edwina stared at him. 'Did you say "sister-
in-law?"' she asked shakily, praying that her ears
had not deceived her.

Damon frowned. 'I don't see why that should
amaze you. She will be my sister-in-law, won't
she?' he demanded, then placed his drink down on
the table again and moved purposefully towards
the still stunned Edwina. 'Now, just you look here,'
he threatened. 'I'm having no shilly-shallying
about this. You're marrying me, got that? I've
given you enough rope, now I'm hauling you in,'

and he matched his threat to the action by pulling her into his arms.

At this point there was a discreet knock on the door before it opened a little way, but Damon shouted, 'Come back in half an hour!' and when the door closed, he proceeded to convince Edwina that he meant what he said.

Not that she needed any convincing! She was sold, hook, line and sinker, and her eyes gave him the answer he was seeking.

A little later on, and held close to him, she told him of her love for him, and why she had acted as she had. 'I didn't think you were serious, and I was afraid of you because of my feelings. You must admit you weren't very nice to me when I tried to apologise about Julia's behaviour, were you?' she said gently.

Damon held her away from him so that he could see her face, flushed now, but with her eyes showing her love for him. 'I guess I got struck at the same time,' he said, with a wry grin. 'I haven't much use for the type of woman I thought I was dealing with, and I'm not in the habit of throwing out those kind of invitations either. I wondered afterwards what the devil had got into me. I only knew I couldn't get you out of my mind. When I couldn't persuade you to come back to the Splendour, I knew I'd have to work harder at it.' He held her close to him again. 'I'm afraid, my love, I still thought you were holding out for higher stakes, and as time went by, I was willing to give in, no matter what you were after. I'd got it pretty bad, you see.'

He was silent for a moment, just content to hold her close, and stroked her silky hair with a gentleness Edwina would not have thought possible for such a man. 'Then there was the Colonel,' he went on. 'At first, I thought he'd got it, too, and I was so damned jealous by then, I assumed that he'd gone overboard for you as well—and of course, there was Knight. But it was the Colonel who made me think again. He might act like an old fuddy-duddy, but he can spot a two-timer a mile away, and he took to you like a duck to water, didn't he?' He drew in a deep breath. 'So, I'd got it all wrong, and I'd a hell of a lot to make up to you. I couldn't force the issue either. I knew you were scared of me, and I began to think it was hopeless. Whatever I tried didn't come off. I thought if I could only get you to spend an evening with me I might be able to dispel some of your fears, and left the rest to providence, only you brought up that damned fictional fiancé!' he growled, shaking her lovingly.

'After that,' he went on in a low voice, 'I didn't see any hope at all. I told myself that I was so infatuated with you that I'd imagined all those signs that I thought I'd seen in your eyes when you thought I wasn't looking at you. The only thing I couldn't do was to forget you, but I thought that as long as you were out of my sight, I'd stand a better chance of recovery.' His lips touched her hair. 'If you only knew what hell it was keeping away from you, with the project so close to the Haven!' He sighed. 'I only wanted to get it over with, and then take off.'

Edwina ran a tender finger over his strong jaw. It didn't matter now, nothing mattered but that it had all come right.

'If it hadn't been for the conference,' Damon continued in a quiet voice, 'I'd still be eating my heart out over you. Can you imagine how I felt when I found you in my room?' he queried, 'and dressed like that?' he added indignantly. 'It was like showing a starving man a banquet, only he couldn't touch a thing!'

Edwina nestled closer to him. 'It was a mistake, Damon,' she said. 'Honestly. The door number was loose.'

Damon chuckled. 'I know,' he said. 'I've stayed at the Consul before. They ought to do something about it.'

Edwina looked at him in amazement. 'You mean you knew all along?' she asked, wide-eyed.

He grinned, and kissed her swiftly. 'Having decided that you were on the level, it was the only answer that made sense,' he said, 'but you can't blame me for trying to capitalise on it, only when it came to it, I couldn't go through with it. Even though I knew you'd marry me after that. You'd feel obliged to, and I haven't sunk that low. I might have wanted you, but not on those terms.'

Going back to that time reminded Edwina of something else. 'Damon,' she asked thoughtfully, 'how did you happen to see that man approach my table? I could have sworn you had your back to me.'

He flicked a wisp of her hair away with a carefree

gesture. 'I knew the minute you came into the room,' he said with an imp of amusement lurking at the back of his eyes. 'And I had you in full view the whole time. There was a mirror, my darling, on the wall facing me, which was probably obscured from you by the crowd. But I saw much more than that,' he added in a deep feeling voice. 'I saw the lovely girl that I adored, watching me with a look in her eyes that belied all that she'd led me to believe. I knew then for certain that you loved me, and I wanted to rush over and take you in my arms. It was as if the room was suddenly flooded with sunlight.' He took a deep breath. 'Only I couldn't. You were engaged, or so I thought. But I was determined to do something about it. Once I knew that you cared for me, nothing, but nothing, was going to keep me away from you. I had to find out more about this Philip, so I tackled Julia.'

There was another tap on the door, a little more hesitant than the last one, but this time Damon bade the waiter enter, and then watched him wheel the trolley out to the balcony. Damon's eyes met Edwina's after the waiter had made his unobtrusive departure. 'You know, I've gone off food,' he said softly. 'I'd much rather we smooched to a record or two.'

Edwina's eyes held a glint of mischief in them as she replied, 'Later. I'm hungry,' but as she saw a certain look in Damon's eyes, she told herself that this was going to be another occasion when she needed that white flag!

Here is a selection of Mills & Boon novels to be published at about the same time as the book you are reading.

HOUSE OF DISCORD	*Jane Arbor*
GREEK ISLAND MAGIC	*Gloria Bevan*
A DEEPER DIMENSION	*Amanda Carpenter*
THE FACE OF THE STRANGER	*Angela Carson*
SERPENT IN PARADISE	*Rosemary Carter*
NEW NURSE AT ST BENEDICT'S	*Lilian Chisholm*
MARRIAGE UNDER FIRE	*Daphne Clair*
A RULING PASSION	*Daphne Clair*
HEART OF GOLD	*Kay Clifford*
GUARDIAN DEVIL	*Linda Comer*
A BAD ENEMY	*Sara Craven*
BURDEN OF RICHES	*Helen Dalzell*
TANGLE OF TORMENT	*Emma Darcy*
THE GATES OF RANGITATAU	*Robyn Donald*
A MISTAKE IN IDENTITY	*Sandra Field*
FALKONE'S PROMISE	*Rebecca Flanders*
A MODERN GIRL	*Rebecca Flanders*
THE PRICE OF FREEDOM	*Alison Fraser*
PROPHECY OF DESIRE	*Claire Harrison*
BEYOND RUBIES	*Rosalie Henaghan*
FOR EVER AND A DAY	*Rosalie Henaghan*
EVER AFTER	*Vanessa James*
GENTLE PERSUASION	*Claudia Jameson*
FORGOTTEN PASSION	*Penny Jordan*
MAN-HATER	*Penny Jordan*
SAVAGE ATONEMENT	*Penny Jordan*
PACIFIC APHRODITE	*Madeleine Ker*
VIRTUOUS LADY	*Madeleine Ker*
DANGEROUS ENCOUNTER	*Flora Kidd*
DARKNESS OF THE HEART	*Charlotte Lamb*
A SECRET INTIMACY	*Charlotte Lamb*
CARIBBEAN CONFUSION	*Mary Lyons*

A GRAND ILLUSION	*Maura McGiveny*
SOUTHERN SAGA	*Miriam Macgregor*
SIROCCO	*Anne Mather*
THE MARRIAGE GAME	*Margaret Mayo*
SPRINGS OF LOVE	*Mary Moore*
THE FAILED MARRIAGE	*Carole Mortimer*
SENSUAL ENCOUNTER	*Carole Mortimer*
SUBTLE REVENGE	*Carole Mortimer*
TRUST IN SUMMER MADNESS	*Carole Mortimer*
VILLA OF VENGEANCE	*Annabel Murray*
THE ROAD TO FOREVER	*Jeneth Murrey*
NEVER TOO LATE	*Betty Neels*
BELOVED STRANGER	*Elizabeth Oldfield*
TAKE IT OR LEAVE IT	*Elizabeth Oldfield*
CHAINS OF REGRET	*Margaret Pargeter*
THE SILVER FLAME	*Margaret Pargeter*
STORM IN THE NIGHT	*Margaret Pargeter*
REMEMBER ME, MY LOVE	*Valerie Parv*
COME LOVE ME	*Lilian Peake*
CASTLE OF THE LION	*Margaret Rome*
RELUCTANT RELATIVE	*Jessica Steele*
TOMORROW—COME SOON	*Jessica Steele*
THE ASHBY AFFAIR	*Lynsey Stevens*
A SPLENDID PASSION	*Avery Thorne*
NEVER TRUST A STRANGER	*Kay Thorpe*
HOUSE OF MEMORIES	*Margaret Way*
ECSTASY	*Anne Weale*
BACKFIRE	*Sally Wentworth*
THE LION ROCK	*Sally Wentworth*
THE TYZAK INHERITANCE	*Nicola West*
WILDTRACK	*Nicola West*
RIDE THE WIND	*Yvonne Whittal*

£5.95 net each